The Young Widow's Trauma

A MYSTERY

by

JAMES I. MCGOVERN

WingSpan Press

Published in the United States and the United Kingdom by WingSpan Press, Livermore, CA

The WingSpan name, logo and colophon are the trademarks of WingSpan Publishing.

ISBN 978-1-63683-005-6 (pbk.)
ISBN 978-1-63683-995-0 (ebk.)

First edition 2021

Printed in the United States of America

www.wingspanpress.com

1 2 3 4 5 6 7 8 9 10

In memory of Margaret F. McGovern (1921-1991)

I.

We met on a bitterly cold evening to make the final decisions on our proposal. Dr. Gruner was late so I sat with John in the Dudleys' rustic living room, Bart and the women bantering in the kitchen. Seven copies of the text to date were arranged on the dining room table through the arched passageway. The radiators were singing but there was heavy frost on the windowpanes.

"A night unfit for man or beast," I commented.

John's eyebrows went up but he stayed reflective, not shifting his gaze to me.

"Could be worse," he said.

"Ah, cliche for cliche."

"They're generally true, notwithstanding."

We again fell silent. A ripple of sophisticated laughter issued from the kitchen.

"For instance," John resumed, "there's hell."

"Perdition down below? Devils and such?"

"No, here on earth. Interwoven with our world. Within our sight and hearing, within a breath."

I said nothing but stared at him, eventually drawing his eyes.

"You recall last month I was off?"

"Yes, your trip. You've been tight-lipped about it."

"There's much I could tell you, but I'm not sure I should. We both might regret it later."

1

I casually looked around.

"It seems we're secure here, John. Please proceed."

"All right."

⸻ ⁂ ⸻

"My ex and I were in Malmo, where she grew up. We'd been there before, of course, in better times. But this time it was different, more–I don't know–oppressive, a yellowish tinge to the gray, the usual gray sky. Not the best place to reconcile, I guess, if that's what we were doing, but we wanted to go back to the start, the beginning, naive though that may sound. She went to see her relatives but I held back. My going didn't seem right, seemed unwise just then. There were friends we both could see, a more promising proposition, and one of them was this guy Sven.

"He had a small farm some distance from town, in a well forested area to the north. He wasn't a true farmer, but he hadn't found his calling by the time his mother died, so he returned to help his father who was there alone. But when the father died soon after it was Sven himself who was alone and isolated. The area is sparsely peopled, almost desolate, very little traffic or commerce. He developed a routine to try to adjust, managing the farm and drawing on transcendent values. But he was still a fairly young man with that troubling absence in his life: the need for a significant other. Pickings were slim where he was living and he'd lost touch with the scene in Malmo, so he decided to go far afield through the matching services. He wound up going farther than he expected, something called the International Pen-Friend League, and more or less fell in with someone very far away, in a country on an island that they share with Indonesia.

"I went out there with my ex the first time, met them

2

couple-to-couple. Rinai, the wife, is quite short, olive complexion and dark hair, which she had in a braid down her back. She was very quiet and conversation was awkward–newlyweds with a divorced couple–so after a while Sven took me out to show me the farm. It was cold with a few flakes blowing around. There wasn't much to see: crops out of season, livestock few, chicken coop unkempt. But he unloaded on me about the marriage. He clearly now saw it as a mistake. The country and culture were totally alien to Rinai. She couldn't begin to adjust. She honored her commitment to him, and he felt attracted to her–deeply, maybe dangerously–but as a couple they had no ties to society, could not function in it beyond subsistence. She had a resentment toward it that might evolve into hostility, which society could well return. Rinai's dark eyes, at first seeming warm and glowing, seemed now to smolder.

"I said to him, 'Perhaps some counseling?' But he dismissed this.

"'She'll have nothing to do with it, any kind. She has her own source of guidance, she says, rooted in her culture.'

"'So what does this involve?'

"'I don't know, really. I hear her murmuring sometimes, chants maybe, or prayers. And she's been in the fields at night. I've watched her. In the stillness I've heard her talking, raising her arms to the sky. Once she lit a small fire. I went to the site next day to see what she'd burned, but there were only nondescript cinders. I puzzled over them, and over what to think of her, but found no answers.'"

⚬┤3⊰⊱

Bart came out from the kitchen and informed us that Dr. Gruner was arriving. John and I got up to take our places at the dining room table. As we riffled through our copies of the proposal, I suggested we have a drink after the meeting. I wanted to hear him finish about Sven and Rinai.

"Sure," he replied, "but I should warn you: There are traumas ahead."

❦

The pub was near-empty on the bitter week night, but we were grateful for the quiet after our tedious meeting. I nursed a stein of dark beer while John went with brandy, thoughtfully rotating his glass on the table. Other voices in the place were low and far from us.

"So then," I ventured, "Sven got himself in a spot. Not that unusual, though, when people are lonely."

"True," John agreed, "but some spots are a lot worse than others. In this case—"

He hesitated, then slowly took a sip, not looking at me.

"The evening after our visit, there was a message for me at the hotel. It was from Sven. He said he needed to see me as soon as possible, extremely important. Wanted me to come back out the next day. I talked it over with my ex. She refused to come with me, seemed to shiver at the thought. She'd been alone with Rinai when I was out with Sven. She hardly touched some food Rinai prepared. I had some myself to be polite, had to admit it was strange."

"So you went by yourself next day?"

"Yes. I found Sven standing outside, not doing anything, just idling it seemed. We didn't go in the house. Instead, he took me around back. To the barnyard. Clouds were heavy, shadows everywhere, so at first I didn't see it. The chicken coop had been burnt to the ground. Completely incinerated, carbonized, scorched earth around it. I could hardly make out

4

the chicken remains. It'd happened in the middle of the night, Sven told me.

"'The light from it woke me up. So bright I thought it was the house.'

"'Shocking, I'll bet. What about Rinai? Did she handle it okay?'

"'She was already up, sitting in the parlor like a statue. She didn't say anything at first, wouldn't respond to me. I got right in front of her, close to her face, stared into those deep, dark eyes. Finally she spoke.'

""'It is as mother said. One time. Way long ago.'"

""'What was it? What did she say?'"

""'A warning comes as fire in the night.'"

"'I was confused, felt anger building, unfocused. I left to see to the fire. I'd seen her in the fields those nights, her own little blaze, the gestures and unintelligible talking. I was suddenly aware that I didn't know her. I'd tried to build a life on quicksand, without a basis for confidence. She's in the house now. I'm settling things down but, I don't know, it could be pretty rough ahead.'

"'This happened the night after our visit. Was there–I hope there wasn't some connection.'

"Sven gave me a knowing look, then shrugged.

"'It's nothing personal. Other people are just a bad fit for her.'

"I suggested we go to the nearest roadhouse for a drink, but Sven declined. He didn't want to leave Rinai alone at the farm. I saw her face at a window–expressionless–as I returned to my car. The visit had been entirely outdoors, in the cold."

⊕⊷3⊶⊹⊱⊷

We had another round of drinks, at John's suggestion. I noticed he'd grown gloomy about the eyes, dully pensive, knew he hadn't told me everything.

"So, why had Sven asked you to return? I mean, why'd he made such a point of it? It was just a chicken coop, after all, and he was speculating about Rinai."

"Yes, I thought so too at the time. I tried to call him as we were leaving Malmo, just to check on things, but there was no answer. Then, when I'm all the way home, I get a couple calls from authorities over there, police and immigration people. They say Sven–well, they say Sven was found dead. What's more, there's *how* he was found. His condition was the same as the chicken coop I saw. He had to be identified through dental records. Terrible. So you see, I'm thinking there was something he couldn't verbalize on that second visit I made. Not to get help, necessarily, but to make sure there was someone who knew what he was facing."

We both attended to our drinks.

"And Rinai?" I queried at length.

"She's being detained for now, her status in the country being reviewed. She's in a nice enough facility–they're quite liberal–no doubt cozier than out on the farm."

"Maybe someone there can help her."

"Well, right now they're working on the criminal case."

"They suspect homicide?"

"Of course. No way it was an accident."

"There's self-immolation."

John's eyes widened.

"Not Sven. He'd gotten off-track a bit but he wasn't suicidal. Anyway, who would do it like that in these times?"

I let it go. Despite our drinking, John was becoming restless.

"Fact is," he continued, "they want me back there for a disposition."

"You?"

"Last one to see him alive, they think, aside from Rinai."

"Think you'll be going?"

He shrugged heavily.

"I'm still undecided but, like them, I'd like to see the thing explained, especially considering the field we're in. And then there's Rinai stuck in limbo."

"It would be quite a credit to you if you could help, and maybe to the new Center we're proposing."

John nodded reflectively.

"My ex won't be coming. Absolute refusal."

"Think you'd be in jeopardy alone? Deemed a suspect like something out of Kafka?"

He managed a smile.

"I doubt it. They're a friendly people, open-minded. But you get on foreign soil and who knows? All the institutions work differently."

"Perhaps Dr. Gruner would be interested."

"No, that's no good. Any negative outcome connected to him would kill the Center. Or else its funding. Same thing."

I looked towards the bar, wondering how late it stayed open, whether we should have another round.

"Would you like to make the trip?" John asked.

I hesitated to refuse, then found I might not. He'd said "like to" and there was no question I'd prefer it, even considering my scheduled duties, co-workers, the clients. All of that could be changed as a sudden necessity, like when a boss on TV tells a secretary to cancel all appointments. Such was my rationalization, alcohol-assisted.

"Of course," I succinctly answered.

❦❖❦

When we arrived in Malmo there were still several days until John's deposition. We could have spent the time sampling the city's attractions, but our interest in Sven and Rinai had grown. John seemed encouraged by my company and wanted to be proactive in studying the case. We decided to visit the Scania district police, who were handling the criminal investigation, the Immigration people being far away in the capital. As an ersatz friend of Sven, we reasoned, John was entitled to some substantial information about the case.

We met with Detective Ulrickson, a young woman who appeared rather delicate for police work. Her senior partner, assigned with her to our case, was occupied with one given higher priority.

"But isn't a likely homicide as bad as it gets?" John asked.

"You might be surprised," she answered. "We know of our reputation for low crime rates, but both the number and nature of crimes here recently worsened."

"So how does this one compare? In seriousness."

"It's–well, it's odd. We haven't been able to get much from her. We tried an interpreter from the Indonesian consulate–her own country doesn't maintain one–but he had no success and didn't want to come back."

"You're still detaining her?"

"Yes, a low-risk facility. We haven't been able to charge her, so it's basically for the Immigration people."

"Will they finish their review soon?"

"I think they're waiting for *us*. It's sort of an impasse. But of course it must be resolved soon."

The detective looked over at me. I hadn't spoken since we were introduced.

"You two are co-workers, then? The same institution?"

"Almost," I answered. "We're starting a new facility, the Center for Integrative Treatment of Extreme Dysfunction. It's awaiting final approval for government funding."

She nodded approvingly.

"We could maybe use your take on our immigrant."

"It's all right if we see her?"

"Well, one of you is a prior acquaintance. So, a personal visit–"

"We'll help any way we can," John said. "By the way, is anyone watching the farm? There were animals–"

"There's a man from the neighboring farm. They were too much for the humane people. We reimburse the neighbor, of course."

It became clear to John and me that the police were not getting far. Their usual procedures were not yielding results. We'd come a long way and were personally invested, as well as extremely curious, so we'd have to make the effort to untangle things ourselves. We left our newly printed business cards as we closed the conversation.

"Thank you, Detective Ulrickson," I said.

"Astrid," she smiled.

❦❧✳❦❧

The relaxed detention for Rinai was in a spacious old mansion on the Baltic coast, panoramic views of the sea and coastline from many windows and balconies. After John parked, we stood a few moments and surveyed the grounds, well wooded and offering serene separation from neighbors and life's complications. It had to be a radical change for Rinai from life on the farm and in her home country.

"Some politicians here," John informed me, "say people commit crimes here just to live better in jail."

We passed a single guard at the ornate entrance and signed in at a desk inside. We waited in the library while Rinai was located and brought to us. I noticed some uneasiness in John, a distracted fidgeting, as if some inner intensity were taking hold. It didn't relax as Rinai was led into the room. She appeared quite at ease, wearing a loose garment of some sort, dark blue, and earrings from which small silver coins dangled. I recognized the coins as being from the eighteenth century.

"We're sorry about your loss," John said. "How are you getting along?"

She nodded without speaking.

"Is there anything you need?"

"No."

"I'd like to ask you about what happened. To see if we can help you."

She was silent. John was concentrating, meeting her gaze as if there were resistance, though to me Rinai was placid.

"After I left you that day, you and Sven on the farm, after the chicken coop burned, can you tell me what happened? Sven was upset, worried about you. Did you talk with him? Was there a plan you made? Please tell me. As a friend who wants to help you."

She looked at him vacantly.

"There was no plan. He was sad."

"Well, did he go over things with you? The fire, what maybe caused it, any problems you were having?"

"We were out of cigarettes."

There was silence. Rinai looked over at me and frowned slightly, retained the frown as she looked back at John, then again at me.

"Would you mind waiting outside?" John asked me.

I waited in the hall until Rinai was led out, then went in to see John. He was reclining thoughtfully in his chair. He watched without expression as I came up and sat down, then he looked away as he spoke.

"It seems there's much more to this than we thought. We may be out of our league."

"Well, we're in a new league anyway. Aren't we, John? 'Extreme Dysfunction?'"

"Yes, that's entirely true. And we're right in the middle of it."

We had dinner within walking distance of our hotel. The sky had darkened early with the air growing rapidly colder. We were as grateful for our drinks as for the food, which was served in generous portions. John had held back about his talk with Rinai, but now loosened up with the assistance of brandy.

"It would be easy to misread her, I think. In many ways. That could well be what got Sven in trouble."

"How do you mean?"

"He probably saw her as most people would: a young innocent in a remote place, disadvantaged, willing to compromise out of a desperate need to escape."

"Was it not that bad for her?"

"From our perspective, maybe it was. But she was no worse off than others in her group, the people she was born into. The country itself is quite small, of course, insignificant on the world stage. And she's from an autonomous region within it, culturally distinct, and from a tribal group within that region, an extended clan, secretive and cultish. Given to odd, perhaps outrageous, practices. I don't know, the language barrier set in. A lot can be lost in translation."

"She seems to trust you, at least. More than myself, anyway. And you only met with her once before, that plus the look through a window."

"Yes, well, the sharing of food can go a long way toward bonding, and she herself prepared it."

"Perhaps another talk with her would reveal more."

John hesitated.

"Actually, there was something more *this* time. I brought up what Sven had told me about her night wanderings, the fire-as-warning idea. It shook her. I knew more than I was supposed to, maybe. She deflected it to her old culture, the microculture. She spoke of something called the Kakili that owns the night, consumes the darkness, must always be honored and appeased to avoid its violent anger. They have

11

ceremonies and sacrifices to accomplish this. The Kakili is accompanied by monsters of a sort, demented humanoids who viciously enforce his slightest angry whim. Rinai's people live within this overarching fear. It permeates their day-to-day lives, even more their night-to-night. They don't know how far the Kakili's power extends. They live in isolation, the few who have left never returning. Rinai is now one of them, but she fears she's been followed by the Kakili or his monsters, doesn't know what they intend for her. They could kill her, she thinks, or force her deportation back to the homeland."

"Does she know how they originated? Where they came from?"

"Lost in antiquity, apparently."

"And they're only around at night."

"Mostly, at least. You have an idea on that?"

"Well, there's a vast array of nocturnal animals. A whole parallel food chain. But she said this character 'consumes the darkness.' Not sure where that would fit in."

"It might have been metaphorical."

"How so?"

"Negative human qualities–ignorance, deceit, lust, hate, avarice, blasphemy, arrogance, you name it. Or, more likely, those who show such qualities."

"That assumes some intelligence, rationality."

"Could be a very low degree. A totally warped perspective."

"Misguided intelligence, ignorant righteousness. We could really get tied up in knots on this, John."

He gave a wry smile.

"Maybe we should stay with the physical facts awhile."

"I fully agree."

"What do you say we visit the farm?"

⊕⊰⊱⊰⊱⊰⊱⊕

We had the advantage of daylight, the portion of it that filtered through the cloud cover. It had been drizzling when we left Malmo but almost let up as we drove. John was at the wheel of our rental as we headed north, through the intensive crops to where they began to thin in favor of dairy farming. Sven's property–now Rinai's–would not be considered prime since it was only marginally arable. Beyond the dairy farms, well to the north, stretched the great forests and lumbering. Beyond that, the tundra. But our business was limited to Scania, slightly inside its border, so we had only a mild sense of leaving mainstream culture behind.

"The route must be getting familiar to you," I said to John.

"Yes. Wish I could say the same about the farm. It wasn't yet a murder site those other times, unless you count the chickens."

As we neared our destination, John drove at reduced speed, pensively watching the empty road ahead. We were both silent. He came to a crescent driveway and pulled in, creeping toward the house through weedy, unkempt grounds. I noticed a goat chewing at plants in a neglected garden.

"Looks like one got out," I said.

"Yes. We'd better have a look in back."

He parked and we got out, I stretching a bit but John striding off at once around the house. I hastened to follow him. I supposed we'd deal with the goat later on.

"Whoa!" I heard John exclaim up ahead.

I joined him in the barnyard, where two cows were standing about looking lost. We also saw that the barn doors stood open. Our main attention, however, was drawn to a scene out in the fields, where a large hog was rooting at something on the ground, joined by a bunch of seagulls. We set off at once toward the action. The ground was soft to muddy from the earlier rain, impeding our progress, but we eventually reached a spectacle that sickened us. The object of the animals' attention had apparently been human, judging from the jeans and boots that mingled with the lower part of the mess, but the upper part had been severely burnt and distorted, as from an explosion or strong gust of flame. Total incineration had been prevented by the rain and wet ground. The scavenging animals had further obliterated the victim's humanity, reducing him to anonymous carrion.

"From the neighboring farm?" I suggested.

"Suppose so," John answered.

He turned away and we took a few steps through the mud. He stopped suddenly and looked at me full.

"But this should get Rinai off the hook."

I said nothing.

"She's been in detention, couldn't have done this, and it's clearly a sequel to the other murder."

I think we should involve the police now, John."

"Right. Do you have your phone?"

"Yes. I don't know the emergency number here but–"

"Call Detective Ulrickson."

<hr />

John gave his deposition next day at the scheduled time. Astrid Ulrickson's partner, Nils Sjoberg, involved himself in the case and sat in on the deposition. She and I sat in the hall and waited, figures on the sideline now. The new victim was in fact a hired man at a neighboring farm. He hadn't been missed since his employer assumed he was dawdling. Our discovery of the body, such as it was, would be included by John in his deposition. While he'd thought this latest death would clear Rinai, there remained the possibility of her involvement in conspiracy.

"She'll remain in detention, then?" I asked Astrid.

"Yes. Anyway, there's the immigration issues."

"We might want to see her again. John, anyway. He's more involved with her from the clinical perspective."

"You're not a therapist yourself?"

"I am. But my primary role at the Center will be assistant to Dr. Gruner, our director."

"Administrative."

"Yes. But I'm also a sort of specialist."

"In extreme cases."

"Well, more specifically in evil. The unredeemed evil one sees in certain unexplained, unforgivable acts of violence or indifference. The negative transcendence towards hell."

"Sounds like some police work."

"Yes, I guess our fields overlap."

"So, what about this case? Have you picked up anything we can maybe use?"

I related Rinai's story of the Kakili, as told to me by John, but also tied it to Sven's account of Rinai's nighttime rituals. Perhaps, I speculated, a lapse in prayer and sacrifice by Rinai was responsible for the heinous killings. The Kakili had been angered.

"You believe that?" Astrid asked.

"In my approach," I answered, "I have to keep a completely open mind. If something exists in the mind of another, on whatever level of reality, it has the power to control that person's actions and the environment around them. The main question is how far that power extends. It can take many forms, some shocking, but the main concern should be its scope and strength, so we can discover how to contain it. In hearing a story like Rinai's, I provisionally accept her explanation until a more standard avenue of thought opens up. The existence of evil is generally accepted as fact, so the embodiment of it in pure form should not be too readily dismissed."

"Your colleague in there, John, he's not saying these same things to them, is he?"

"No. His approach is mostly conventional. He's just giving his observations and background on Sven."

She exhaled with a hint of relief, and I guessed incredulity.

"Look, I don't mind if you're skeptical."

She looked surprised.

"No, there have been cases where I could pretty much see what you're talking about."

"Just without the Kakili?"

"Well, maybe with a humanoid or two like those with him."

We exchanged smiles, hints of attraction growing from our shared knowledge of evil.

⊶⧓⧗⧓⊷

We had dinner that night at a restaurant suggested by Astrid. John left the table to call Dr. Gruner from the lounge, our time zone difference making it necessary. The doctor was difficult to reach aside from limited hours.

"The conversation is a long one," Astrid commented.

"He's apprising Dr. Gruner of developments. The doctor is apparently taking an interest."

John showed a satisfied smile on his return.

"Our proposal has been accepted, no major revisions. Funding to commence forthwith."

"That's great!"

"Congratulations," Astrid added.

"They're moving forward with the office and support staff, publicity still an issue. He thinks Rinai's case could be a signature achievement, a real credential, but there's her relocation to negotiate."

"Problems with security and such?"

"Well, he has connections, thinks he can do medical necessity on his end. But the authorities here, of course, might have other issues."

I turned to Astrid.

"What do you think?"

"You mean, take her to your clinic, to America?"

"Yes."

She gave a bemused smile.

"I don't know. I wouldn't have much to say about it. Even on our investigation, Nils is taking over."

"Is he reasonable?"

"Usually, yes. Although he had mixed feelings about your interview of Rinai. Thought we ourselves should have gotten the Kakili story. I don't think he'd want you to see her again. Until he's finished himself, I mean."

"What about the farm?" John asked. "Is that off-limits, too?"

"Well, the tape is down, the animals boarded up north. The house is locked up, though."

"Do you have a key? I'd really like to have another look at it. Refresh my memory for Dr. Gruner."

Astrid looked down.

"I'm afraid I gave it to Nils. But hold on—"

She dug into her handbag, brought out a slim metal tool, turned it in the candlelight so it glinted.

"Do you know how to use one of these?"

"I've had some experience," I said, John giving me a look. Astrid handed me the pick.

"Just be sure to lock up when you leave."

<hr />

There had been moments of sunlight while we were still at the hotel, but once on the road we had the familiar cloud cover. Mile after dismal mile, we were still buoyed by a sense of purpose but the forces against us were daunting. Dr. Gruner was encouraging, as well as ambitious, but did he appreciate the nature of this problem and the degree to which he relied on our initiative?

"What do you hope to find?" I asked John.

"Oh, nothing conclusive," he said. "The police would pick up on something like that. But maybe just a hint in the general layout, some idiosyncrasy, something out of place, a break in the barrier between a human mind and delusion."

"Thus bringing it within the range of therapy."

"Yes, more or less."

As we came to the farm I was struck again by the grayness and quiet of the surrounding countryside, even more pronounced than on my earlier visit. There was no goat in the garden this time, or other animals, and vegetation had slipped into deeper dormancy or death. We parked to one side of the house and approached the rear door, guessing it might be easier to enter. I brought out the lock pick furnished by Astrid and commenced to examine my project. As I did so, however, trying the knob, the door moved inward since the lock had not been engaged.

"Convenient," John commented.

"Best be quiet," I warned.

We entered gingerly, stood listening in a modest kitchen. We tried a few hellos and John an "official business." Getting no response, we proceeded through the rooms, finding mild disorder but no unusual objects or situations. John stood in consternation.

"I'm sure she had artifacts from her culture on the walls and shelves. And did you notice how little food there was in the kitchen?"

"Yes."

But it occurred to me that I hadn't been looking at things as closely as John. I hadn't given him the full benefit of a second set of eyes.

"Think I'll have another look upstairs," I said, and up I went.

The main bedroom looked out from the front of the house, over the unkempt grounds to the road beyond. It had the same lived-in look as downstairs. I checked under the mattress and behind the bureau and a cabinet, then thoroughly in the closet. Nothing unusual. The two back bedrooms were scantily furnished and dusty, apparently long disused. I noticed, however, that the bedspread in one was not as tightly or tidily tucked as the other. Closer inspection revealed a bit of rumpling. Raising my eyes, I noticed a small, whitish object on the floor on the far side of the bed, near the window looking out over the barnyard and fields. I went over and picked it up, found it to be a small animal tusk, or perhaps a large tooth, with a hole neatly bored in it for cord or chain. It currently had a fine thread looped through it, possibly for hanging from the small tack I saw at the top of the window frame. A hard window closing could have jarred it loose.

Suddenly, I was distracted by movement out the window. John was walking out through the barnyard, toward the fields and a figure standing in the remains of crops. The figure was obscure with the overcast, but seemed shaggy in nondescript clothing, quite tall in comparison to John as he approached. I saw my colleague begin to speak, getting little or no response from the other party. As John persisted, the other apparently said something as he pointed with his left arm over the countryside. John turned his head to look in the indicated direction while the tall one raised his right arm, holding a long object. There was a blur of motion my vision couldn't follow but my next registered image was of John's body, headless, slumping forward onto the ground. I next saw the assailant looking toward the house, past it to the parked car, then lumbering off into the fields, but not in the direction he'd been pointing.

Within myself, as I stood horrified, my rationality struggled for a course of action. Bolt the door, I thought, the sliding inside bolt, and gain a weapon from the kitchen, the largest knife, or was there an axe somewhere? But the attacker had gone, was going anyway, and a phone was on the kitchen wall.

I hastened from the room and down the stairs I'd just ascended, John then much alive and still with me. The emergency number, 1-1-2, was posted on the wall phone. Immediately, forcefully, I punched it in.

II.

Nils was a large man, unsuited to the plastic chairs of the interview room. He was the one with many papers, the notes and reports on John's demise and the incidents leading up to it, as well as some follow-up on John's killer. There remained the questions about Rinai's future and, overlapping them, speculation about her involvement with the Center for Integrative Treatment of Extreme Dysfunction. Dr. Gruner's interest in her was unflagging, decisively surviving his dismay and sorrow upon learning of John's fate.

Nils was at the head of the table, Astrid and I on either side with far fewer papers.

"Very sketchy on the fugitive," Nils said. "Tramp had him on a freight train headed north, but it was deep in timber country by then. We couldn't nab him at a stop. He'll likely try an escape over the frozen portion of bay, get out of our jurisdiction. It's risky out there since the ice is still thickening. Best we can do is alert the Finns."

"You couldn't use a helicopter?" I asked. "Search and Rescue dropping him a cable or ladder or something?"

"They have to want it for that to work," Astrid answered. "This one wants to elude us."

"Also, our people would be vulnerable," Nils added. "He could have a gun. Landing is out of the question, of course.

But he might just fall through the ice himself, make things easy for us."

"Not for John," I found myself saying, "unfortunately."

"Right," Nils acknowledged, and looked down at his papers. "But where do we stand now with Rinai?"

Astrid glanced at her notes.

"Immigration has received a statement of medical necessity from Dr. Gruner in America. They say that, if the police inquiry is closed, she'll be allowed to travel there if her doctor here signs off."

"I believe the two doctors have consulted," I added.

Nils nodded thoughtfully.

"Well, we really shouldn't hold her longer, and returning her to the farm seems problematic, but putting her on a plane to yet another country, I don't know. It wouldn't be by herself, would it?"

His eyes moved in my direction. I felt the absence of John, his taking the lead on this. My duty to Dr. Gruner suddenly weighed heavily.

"I can accompany her," I stated flatly.

The other man's eyes narrowed.

"You have no female staff here?"

"No, I'm afraid not. Someone could meet us on arrival, of course."

"I can make the trip," Astrid interjected. "It will provide a positive closing for our involvement with her."

Nils thought for a moment.

"I'll run it by the captain."

❦

Astrid accompanied me through the details of receiving John's remains. Dr. Gruner had been unable to locate relatives,

22

so he asked Bart Dudley to approach the ex-wife, but Bart reported she was unable or unwilling to get involved. I therefore had to arrange a local cremation and bring the ashes back with me on returning to America, along with Rinai as a patient. I felt especially fortunate that Astrid would continue to be my companion.

"Quite a day," she remarked later.

We were in her apartment after dinner in a bistro, our first together since the one with John.

"Yes," I said. "They're increasingly full."

"Shall we have a liqueur?"

"Yes."

She served it in two tiny glasses and we settled on her couch.

"So terrible about John," she said. "Has it fully sunk in for you, do you think? Sometimes the initial shock serves to protect, to stun a person against the full reality. At least I find it that way in my work."

"I don't know," I replied. "I find myself thinking, if only he'd held back, been more cautious, not gone walking right out there. But he was so intent on finding something that it seems his perspective narrowed. He forgot about safety."

"And he wasn't you."

Our eyes met. She moved closer and took my hand. A sudden memory struck me.

"Right, but you know what? The odd thing is, I was the one who found something. It's still in my coat over there. I picked it up just before I saw John killed."

I got up to fetch the object, leaving Astrid bemused, then brought it back close to her on the couch. We looked at it together, she turning it in her hand.

"A tooth from an animal, a large one, or else a tusk? Used as a charm or jewelry I guess, judging from the hole."

"It was next to a bed that looked slept in, or *on* anyway. In one of the spare bedrooms, after the police sweep."

"So a squatter then, maybe our suspect."

"I guess I should have turned it in."

"Oh, I don't know." She laid the object on her coffee table. "I don't see how it would change anything."

She re-took my hand. I thought back to where we'd left off, met her inviting eyes.

"No, I guess it wouldn't."

As we kissed and I brushed her dark hair back from her face, I noticed that it was lighter at the roots.

"I see you're a blonde. Golden concealed by solid brown."

"It lends me some gravitas for the job. Blondes are very common here."

My hand on her far shoulder conveyed its smallness, though it was firm, presumably strong.

"You know, from your build, one wouldn't guess you're a police officer."

She gave a little shrug.

"Things often aren't what they seem, Mr. Investigator. "

"Yes." A pause, then: "So you'll be all right, you think, on the plane with Rinai?"

"Of course!"

She took my head in both hands and kissed me hard. An aggressive move meant to be reassuring, I thought. As we parted, though, and she silently looked in my eyes, it was a mutual and simultaneous emotion that guided us forward. It wasn't until much later, on our backs in her bed, moonlight through the window, that we spoke in sentences again.

"The sky has cleared."

"Not for long, I expect."

"So how did you get into police work?"

"It was in my family. My father thought my brother would be joining him on the force, but Edvin had a college friend whose father ran a NEVS dealership, formerly Saab. They offered Edvin a job and he went to work there with his friend.

I was close to my father, always curious about his job, so I decided to fill the gap."

"Your father must have been pleased."

"Very much so. Though he can be overprotective toward me. Got me partnered with Nils, who can be quite controlling. Another protective sort. What about you, your 'specialty?' How did that come to be?"

"It was probably always in my nature. But the turning point came on my visit to a lost culture, a supposed shortcut to my doctorate in anthropology. My advisor, an aging full professor, recommended it, something he wanted to do himself but wasn't up to. He'd enjoy the trip vicariously through me, his protégé. Anyhow, the tribal folks lived on one of the lesser islands of the Philippines, inland through some jungle, up in the hills. I had a guide who'd learned their language a little. I did the usual academic stuff, observing their customs and relationships, what I could get of their history, found them rather dull at first. But then one of them, a precocious teenage girl, offered to show me something special, a subgroup of the tribe, required to live some distance away. My guide was against it and would not come with us.

"'We should leave them alone,' he said, 'shun them as these people do. The threat they are to this village is doubly so for us. We are outsiders.'

"'But surely it's just some superstition.'

"'One should never underestimate evil.'

"I thanked him for his warning but of course I went with the girl. I'd come too far to return to my advisor with pablum. The girl led me along a winding path as evening set in, the only time available since I had to depart next day. We came to a disorderly hamlet, shacks scattered in an area that was more beaten down than cleared. The surprised inhabitants scrutinized me, then pulled me into their circle of activity. To one side I saw an old woman stirring a pot. She grinned at me and spooned up a large beetle amid the steam. I also noticed a bat wing protruding from the mix. I'd apparently interrupted a performance in which a naked couple now resumed snarling and clawing at each other prior to having mutual oral intercourse. There were children watching, though not so many in relation to the number of adults. There was no music despite the presence of a bored looking man with a drum before him.

"'You must stay brave now,' said the girl guiding me.

"A boy and a girl, children, were brought forward. The old woman I'd seen spooned some liquid out of the pot, swirled it in a cup and blew on it, handed it to the boy who was induced to drink. He seemed unfazed. The girl also received the cup but barely touched her lips. The man with the drum began beating a rhythm but was soon interrupted by a middle-aged man who rose and looked over at me. He dismissed the children and spoke to my companion in their tribal language.

"'Instead of children,' she translated, '*you* will see into the cobra, very close, see its power, gain the power into you. Or you may drink the old hag's soup and leave.'

"'I will take the cobra.'

"'The soup is boiled, no harm to you.'

"'No. I want the cobra.'

"I was young, of course, prone to recklessness, my disgust at the soup not helping. A man appeared holding the snake, smaller than I expected but quick-looking, its jaws held shut by the man's thumb and forefinger. The man slipped behind me—we were standing—and held the snake suspended around my head at eye level, its tail visible to my right, its glaring head just a little to my left. Its flicking tongue was maybe eight inches from my face. I met its stare, willfully ignoring the bright green of its forked tongue against the onyx of its skin. The fellow with the drum was providing a staccato rhythm. That too I ignored as I probed the snake's inner workings through its uncompromising eyes, the one-dimensional drive to inflict death restrained only by the erratic fingers of a feckless human. I saw the contempt for mercy, for compassion, the antithesis of love, a negative transcendence extending infinitely far through a universe of unmitigated evil. I felt a caving within me as the knowledge of ultimate power took hold. As the man holding the cobra grew tired, finally withdrawing it, I felt gratitude not only for escape but for the unholy wealth of my experience. I'd met the ultimate intent for destruction, the reflexive forbidding of existence, after which all other threats are weak echoes."

I paused, looked over at Astrid beside me. Her eyes were toward the ceiling, a soft glisten of moonlight on them.

"There was more, but that's mainly what put me on my path."

"Well, I'm glad you got out okay. By whatever means."

"Oh, that was never a problem. Money was changing hands."

"What I meant was, I'm glad you can be here with me. Now. That you're alive and here beside me."

I reached out and touched her, forgot everything except her face as it turned to me, the moonlight giving way to shadow.

⊷⊷⊹⊱⊰⊹⊱⊰

The domestic flight to the capital went pretty well. Rinai hardly spoke, but we'd come to understand that she only spoke willingly in one-to-one conversations. She was otherwise withdrawn, seemingly content to let events bear her forward, in this case across the Atlantic to a status of extreme dysfunction patient. Our second flight would take six hours, but Rinai appeared comfortable in her business class window seat. Astrid and I were in two adjoining seats in the middle, across an aisle from Rinai, with a vacant window seat to my left, across another aisle. The business class seats were about half full, economy class much fuller. Dinner had been served and we were resting in dimmed lighting when Astrid's voice interrupted my slumber.

"She's been in there a very long time."

"What? Where?"

"The restroom, of course. The one on her side."

"Has anyone complained?"

"No. There's the other one and not many people here."

"So, what do you think?"

"Well, maybe we could ask the stewardess–"

"No. We'd better not. We don't want to get into explanations."

Astrid hesitated, glancing back toward the restroom.

"Okay. But what, then?"

"How about you give her a knock yourself? People do that, I think. Check on a friend who maybe fell asleep there?"

Astrid said nothing but got up to do the task. In the quiet of the sleeping plane, I heard her small, distant knock and muffled supplication. Soon she had slipped back into her seat.

"She made a noise, maybe said something. I couldn't make it out."

"Any distress?"

"No."

"All right, then. We're good."

We'd hardly spoken before Rinai came back, resumed her seat, and closed her eyes without comment. I noticed a light sheen of perspiration on her and a slight tic about her eyes and the corners of her mouth. These faded as she settled into sleep. Astrid seemed unconcerned so I let it go. We joined the rest of the passengers trying to sleep away the hours. As I was departing consciousness, however, I became remotely aware of a disturbance to my right. I grudgingly focused on the noise, forcing myself to sit up and gaze beyond Astrid , whose eyes were now first fluttering open. Rinai was still in deep slumber.

"Help! Can someone please help?" a woman was shouting. "This man needs help here!"

Astrid dazedly sat up. I stood to look beyond her, saw the woman a bit down the aisle on Rinai's side, frantically looking around. She was standing over the man who'd been sitting behind Rinai, the man now lying in the aisle and thrashing wildly, a reddish foam spilling from his mouth.

"He's dying!" the woman shouted. "Someone help him!"

I started to work my way past Astrid but was preempted by crew members arriving. They hesitated on seeing the convulsions, the foam, but then the lead stewardess moved in to use CPR, a male steward trying to pin the flailing arms. I myself grabbed a whipping leg, taking a blow to my face but sparing the stewardess. Another stewardess was calling for a doctor from among the passengers. After some delay, a man about ninety was assisted up from economy. He gingerly bent down to examine the stricken man, who was now still. The plane's copilot arrived and hovered over the now subdued scene. After meticulous examination of the stricken man, the old doctor rose with a quizzical expression.

"This man is dead," he informed the copilot.

The copilot grunted and turned to the lead stewardess.

"I'll ask the captain about divergence." Then, noticing Rinai still asleep amid the scene: "What's wrong with that woman? Is she drunk?"

"She's with us," Astrid spoke up.

She flashed her Scania police badge, also laying her hand on my arm. The copilot grunted and turned to leave. People started backing away, the lead stewardess instructing her colleagues to bring blankets and clear out a corner of business class. The male steward was assigned to get the body into the corner seat, strapped in and blanketed.

"Can you help with the body, officer?" he asked me.

I nodded without comment and joined him in the effort.

Astrid turned her attention to Rinai, speaking her name and shaking her to elicit consciousness. Moving the body was no small task, narrow spaces and sharp turns increasing the need to hold our burden aloft. Its weight and awkward form tended to frustrate our efforts. It was eventually in place, the aisle cleaned up, everyone settled, but the cause of the man's demise had somehow escaped discussion.

Astrid and Rinai were having colas when I rejoined them, a small bottle of whiskey awaiting myself, next to a cup of ice. I immediately poured out my beverage, took a satisfying sip, noticed a turbaned man now occupying the seat to my left, across the aisle. He was doubtless one of those moved to isolate the corpse. Gazing past Astrid, I saw Rinai on the far right looking calm and relaxed, though she and Astrid were not speaking. The man on my left was peering into a tiny book, likely a religious text, so our row was momentarily silent.

"You're not having wine?" I said to Astrid.

"It seems I'm on duty. Or should I say *we* are?"

"Well, it was definitely a job."

"Yes."

"So," I lowered my voice, "you talked with Rinai?"

"A little. Asked how she was, told her what happened. She seemed indifferent, just asked if he'd been rich, the dead man. Told her I didn't know, of course, or anything else about him."

"What do you make of her sleeping? With all that going on?"

"I don't know. Weird. Although babies do it sometimes."

"An infantile state of mind."

"I saw no sign of drug influence."

"Perhaps induced some other way."

"By whom? We're on this plane."

"Perhaps herself."

Astrid thought a moment.

"She *was* in the restroom a long time."

"Maybe you could have a look in there."

"Why me? It's unisex."

"It's on your side."

Astrid gave me a look.

"I'm here as an official courtesy, Mr. Investigator. An escort. Our case on Rinai is closed."

"Oh, yeah. I forgot."

She gave me a peck on the cheek to sweeten the pill. I thought the man in the turban glanced over, though I couldn't be sure.

❈

I wasn't rushed in my inspection of the restroom. It was one of two in business class, which was only half full and closed to economy passengers, and we still flew in darkness. After a general perusal, I checked for hidden corners and places of concealment, considered probing the trash bin. I pulled out the liner and checked the contents, but there was nothing unusual. I examined the sink, the toilet, then the surfaces around them. Everything was surprisingly clean, as if passengers were wiping things down after usage. To one side of the sink, however, near an outer edge of the flat area, I noticed a spot of scuffing on the surface. It had to be recent since it was atop the recent water pattern from wiping. It was a small mass of even tinier marks that suggested the crushing of a roundish object, pea to marble size. I therefore directed my eyes over the edge of the sink top to the floor immediately beneath where, on close examination, I discovered a dark greenish powder that had escaped my earlier perusal.

By the time I left the restroom, I'd collected the powder from the floor on a damp paper towel, the best I could do, and folded it into my shirt pocket. The dampness raised a scent that I'd noticed on entering the restroom, an acrid vegetable

31

smell that I'd assumed was disinfectant. On returning to my seat, I found Astrid drowsy but not asleep, so I asked her to check on Rinai.

"While you're at it, can you see how many earrings she's wearing?"

"Why?"

"I'll tell you later."

She got up and stepped across the aisle, got no response to speaking Rinai's name.

"She's fine," Astrid said on returning, "and one earring, left ear."

"Small greenish stone?"

"Yes, suspended. A little globe."

"Didn't she have two before?"

"Before when?"

"Prior to the man dying, and to her taking so long in the restroom."

Astrid thought a moment.

"Yes, I think so."

"Ah."

She waited expectantly for my explanation, now fully alert. I related my examination of the restroom, ending with a pat to my shirt pocket, Astrid declining a whiff of the green powder.

"So then," she whispered, "there was grinding of the other earring, the stone part, not really a stone, with the resulting powder somehow causing the man's death. Is that it?"

"Well, partially. There's obviously some missing details."

"Yes, there are. So what do you want to do?"

"Watch her closely. Keep her away from other people. Get her to the Center, a controlled environment. She's a dysfunctional if there ever was one."

We were met on our arrival by Bart and Helen Dudley, their greetings subdued by my conveyance of John's ashes.

"Dr. Gruner wanted to come himself," Bart related, "but he was busy getting things ready for Rinai."

"At the Center?" I asked. "It's already open?"

"Pretty much. The corrections people left it in good shape."

The building being converted had housed young female offenders pending dispositions on their cases. With the proportional increase in female crime, a larger facility had been needed. The existing one, however, was ideally suited to our plans for a secure, semi-residential treatment center.

"Welcome to the United States," Helen said to Rinai.

"I'm tired," Rinai answered. "The trip was bad."

"A man passed away en route," Astrid explained.

We collected Rinai's luggage and left the airport in a car emblazoned with the Center's acronym, CITED. Rinai was in the middle of the back seat and slumped heavily against me, asleep, before we'd gotten very far. Astrid, on the other end, stared into the winter scenery of a country new to her. Bart was at the wheel with Helen next to him in the passenger seat.

"We'll be having a memorial service for John," Helen said over her shoulder.

"That will be nice," I responded.

"Any new developments on, you know, the culprit?"

"They think he left the country."

I wasn't about to discuss it further, not with Rinai in the car. Helen might have sensed this. She was a gentle, compassionate woman, long dark hair and glasses.

"We'll invite John's ex, of course, but I don't know if she'll come. His file had a brother listed as emergency contact, but he didn't respond to our messages."

"Perhaps we were the ones closest to him."

"Yes," Helen agreed sadly.

We arrived at our destination, a low, functional building in dark brown brick, set among mature trees and grassy knolls, now brown with winter. As we awakened Rinai and exited the car, Dr. Gruner appeared with Midori and an imposing security guard. The director was beaming at our successful delivery of a prize client, oblivious for now to the costs involved. As introductions concluded and we moved to escape the cold, I drew Midori aside and reached inside my coat.

"I need to get something analyzed."

"A paper towel?"

"No, there's a dark green powder in the folds."

"Organic?"

"I'm not sure."

"It helps if you use an evidence pouch."

"Yes, ma'am. It was unexpected, a surprise."

"Lucky you."

"Oh, and there's something else."

I dug in my pockets and brought out the little tusk or big tooth from Sven's farm.

"This might be out of my field."

"Well, we *did* all agree to be versatile."

"Yes, sir. And will that be all?"

"Yes, except I really look forward to working with you."

She carefully wrapped the items in clean tissues as we followed the others into the building.

⊖⊷⊰⊱⊹⊱⊰⊶⊝

With Rinai accepted at the Center, Astrid and I withdrew and taxied to my apartment. My detective friend's work was done and she'd be expected back rather promptly. I was hoping, though, that some latitude might be gained, some opening in the rush of events that would allow our relationship to grow. I sensed she wanted it too but I delayed bringing it up, let it

34

hang in the air between us to sweeten the evening and night ahead. On our own without the others, we relaxed in each other's arms, yet we couldn't escape the brutal reality of our work, the looming harshness of its demands.

"Another day, another night, then I should leave," she said. "They'll be hassling Nils."

"He's a big boy. He can handle them."

"But not all the cases. Not for long."

"No, I suppose not."

"I'll still love you, though. Long distance."

I smiled, mostly from amusement. It wasn't something I believed in. But I kissed her as she looked past me.

"You think they'll be all right? There at the Center? They don't know her, after all. Not like we do."

"Helen and Rachel are there tonight, plus a guard. Regular night staff is starting soon."

"That thing on the plane, I don't know. I have a bad feeling about it. She showed no emotion when I woke her, told her about the man, when you were off with the steward and the body. Just that idle question she asked, 'Was he rich?'"

"But that's what we're into, Astrid, don't you see? You in your work sometimes, me in my own most always. The evil that exists in people's hearts, their souls, the effects when it rears its ugly head in their actions. I've seen it and you know it, too. We can't run from it but not because it controls us. It's because we don't want to."

She looked at me silently for a moment, then looked away.

"That story you were telling me about the tribe, the one you studied. That was near where Rinai is from, wasn't it?"

"Well, a different country. But just a stretch of water between. Reachable by outrigger on a good day."

"Tell me more about that night, after you eyeballed the cobra. What else happened?"

"Something nasty. You might regret hearing about it."

"Tell me anyway."

"All right." But I hesitated, recalling the scene reluctantly. "There was a period of some confusion, anticipation among the people gathered, then an approaching disturbance from back among the huts. A group of several men entered the clearing, leading on strong ropes a tall and heavy creature, very dirty and shaggy, with many old wounds and some recent. The people had grown excited and some tried to approach the creature but were waved away with flaming clubs. A drumbeat began and the middle-aged man who seemed to be in charge distributed pointed sticks to select individuals. He glanced at me as if considering, but refrained from giving me a stick. The people who had them, maybe six or seven, were soon poking them at the creature, raising snarls of anger, then howls of pain. They weren't quite spears but they were causing fresh wounds. The people observing were laughing and hooting, except the men with the ropes who were straining themselves. I'd been nagged by the thought that the creature might be human but I saw now that it didn't matter. Suffering is suffering, by whatever victim. It's pure, fungible.

"'We go when this ends,' the girl with me said.

"The older man shouted an order and the creature's harassers retreated. The old woman was there again with her foul stew. She offered it to the creature, who was cowering now but who rose up and seized the pot with both hands, raised it high and gulped down the disgusting contents, the bat wing and a beetle or two spilling off onto the ground. A collective gasp went up from the crowd and they raised their arms to the sky, then bowed to the ground facing the creature. I went down too to avoid standing out, at least I think that was the reason, and the girl came down next to me.

"'We must go now. Come.'

"We got up and slipped away, and I followed her back to the village proper. An odd feeling of reluctance was with me.

My official guide was relieved to see me back. He found me rather distant, I guess, and it took me a while to start thinking academically again. I was changed."

"And are you still?" Astrid asked.

I looked at her in the near-darkness, amid the bedclothes.

"Some things stay with you. Not only in memory. In other ways as well. Penetrating. Overriding. Know what I mean?"

"Yes."

I studied her closely, traced one side of her face.

"How about you quit your job and stay here?"

"No."

"So, what then?"

"It only takes a plane ride now and then. We take turns."

We both slept peacefully later, despite the horrors we involved ourselves in and discussed. It wasn't that we were hardened against them, grown callous. It was more that they provided a matrix of understanding through which we ordered and understood the world: its people and events, its dangers, the actions and random devastation that could obliterate goodness and beauty at any time. We couldn't stop it, couldn't always avoid it, but we could lessen its damage, and doubly so together.

III.

Ididn't report to the Center the day after my return, rather spending the day with Astrid with the blessing of Dr. Gruner. Her flight was the following morning, the time until then all our own, though Midori called toward evening with some of the information I'd wanted.

"It appears entirely organic," she said. "I've identified rue, sage, henbane, and belladonna. A rather exotic mix. Larger sample might show animal fragments."

"Some kind of herbal medicine?"

"The combination doesn't match any folk remedies. The substances share a characteristic, though."

"What's that?"

"They're all used in ceremonies or sacrifices involving evil spirits, the devil and such. But there are many other favored ingredients, maybe even where you got this stuff."

"I see. Good work, Midori. What about the tusk?"

"I shipped it by overnight to the college lab. Couldn't match it myself, but a specialist will."

"Okay, we'll wait on that. I owe you a coffee."

"Oh, can we accept gratuities?"

"I'll make an exception for you."

"You're so nice."

Her findings were of course disconcerting, raising dark

images of what we were dealing with. Dr. Gruner would have to be apprised, of course, and I could mention the findings to Astrid, but otherwise as few people as possible should know, I thought. Things could easily fly off-track, breed unscientific hysteria. The case of Rinai and our success with it would be the cornerstone of our institution. We had to be seen as rational, uncompromising scientists, worthy of society's trust in tackling its most extreme negative behaviors.

━━⊰⊱✶⊰⊱━━

Dr. Gruner was at the work table in his office, his expression somewhere between pensiveness and consternation. A scattering of correspondence lay before him, along with folders, markers, paper clips and such. He greeted me briefly as I entered and gestured toward a chair opposite.

"You had a restful day, I hope?"

"Oh, yes. Good to go, as they say."

"Our client rested well, too. Slept most of the day, in fact. I had Rachel stay with her. I'm thinking of leaving it that way, a permanent assignment."

I was a bit surprised.

"You don't think Helen, with her experience–?"

"I've a sense the lead worker will need to exert firmness at times. Rachel has the edge on that. It would've been John's case, after all. Speaking of which, we need to replace him ASAP. It will be difficult, not like hiring support staff."

He waved vaguely toward the door to the hallway.

"Yes," I agreed. "He was a major loss."

"As for Helen, she'll be busy soon enough with our number two client, now being determined."

He gestured at the clutter on his table.

"The press release brought substantial response.

39

Unfortunately, quantity was not matched by—well, appropriateness. Referrals for common criminals, or for people with everyday problems, or else not everyday but by no means *extreme*."

"Are there any we can use?"

"I put aside a few. Helen's case will have to be drawn from them. We *do* need to build a clientele. There's this fire-starter boy out east. Only fourth grade, standard therapies ineffective. Then there's this older boy they found, severe neglect apparently. Non-verbal, won't keep any clothes on, coils up like a snake and strikes out like one when approached. Promising. Not for Helen, though. She might do well with this mother who killed her own children. Some complexity to it, knots to untie, not just another lawyer ploy. If we prefer the lighter side, something to balance Rinai, there's this senior lady who keeps sneaking onto planes without a ticket. Or, for some confidential work, a high state official who can't keep from shoplifting in discount stores. There's an odd one."

He dropped the papers resignedly and sat back.

"So, what do you think?"

I met the expectant stare, intensified through horn-rimmed glasses. His face was wide, topped by rather oily curly hair. He wore a tweed suit this day.

"Well," I answered, "I suppose the mother who killed her children."

"For Helen."

"Yes."

"Alright, that's done. Now," he came forward, "getting back to Rinai, I'd like for Rachel to report directly to you, with the understanding—Rachel's and Rinai herself—that you have full final authority in the case. I'll be quite busy with administrative matters and, frankly, I think you're more closely attuned to the reality that is Rinai than I myself am."

"It'll be done, doctor."

"Terrible about John. I admire the way you handled it. Thank you. The best way to honor his memory, I think, is to make this case a catalyst for the success of the Center. To gain something positive from such horror has to be the best response to it, and I think your expertise will get us there. I trust you."

Dr. Gruner, I discovered, was even busier with administrative matters than he'd let on. In addition to the facility and staff issues, he was working to obtain further endowments and public funding. Various events and traveling were involved, so he was not a dependable presence at the Center. I was therefore thrust into more of a leadership role than I savored. I mentioned to Bart that I'd thought we had firm financial footing, whereupon he admitted it had been "puffed" a bit to gain approval for the proposal. It appeared the slowness in hiring staff had been more of a necessity than poor planning.

"I'm sure he'll be bringing in support," Bart said. "People are more generous at Christmas."

The holidays were in fact upon us, though for me it meant an even greater role. Dr. Gruner was well known for his gregariousness, his enjoyment of festivities and involvement with his communities, so his absence from the Center became a norm. I was thus, for the season, the regular overseer of a quiet, near-empty facility. Rachel attended to Rinai, engaging her in activities and trying to establish rapport, the security guards made their rounds, but others were not around much. Most of the support staff was starting after New Year's, though a psychiatric nurse would begin a few days earlier, coinciding with the arrival of Helen's assigned client, the mother/child-killer.

I was in my office on Christmas Eve when Midori called from her home. She'd gotten feedback from the college lab about the tusk or large tooth.

"It comes from a babirusa," she said, "a wild pig in Indonesia. It's very old, possibly an extinct sub-species. The babirusa has upper and lower tusks, both pointed up. Yours is a lower, they're smaller. The upper ones curve back as they grow, even to the point where they pierce the animal's skull."

"That's a nice image for Christmas Eve. How could they possibly evolve that way?"

"I don't know, but they've been around forever. One of the earliest know mammals. Ugly but adaptable."

"Like most of my friends, present phone caller excepted."

"Oh, so we're friends then?"

"Of course, Midori. And I owe you a lunch. No, make it a dinner."

"Just so it's not wild pig."

<hr />

I arranged for a night matron to report after Christmas, rather than with the new year, this to relieve Rachel in her supervision of Rinai. Helen had been giving her colleague some respite, but I wanted both of them at full strength for their regular duties. Helen's killer client was about to arrive, along with two additional security guards which, with the one added for Rinai, gave us a total of four. I asked Bart how the extra guards would impact our budget, but he said the referring state would be picking up the tab.

"Do you have it in writing?" I asked. "In a contract?"

"Dr. Gruner made the arrangements. He said they'd be paying since it was their requirement."

My silence must have suggested skepticism.

"Look," he continued, "this case is a cash cow. Not like your foreign job, a big drain."

"Actually, it was John brought the case in."

"Okay, John's big drain."

I let it go. I needed Bart. I had no taste for the nitty-gritty of financial and legal matters. I also had to remember we were talking about his wife's client, her first one with the Center. And Bart himself would be needed to service a client now and then, assuming the Center didn't flop.

Helen's client arrived as scheduled, wearing manacles that were removed in the lobby. She was tallish with limp dark hair, oversized glasses, and a vapid look. Helen took charge of her and extended a warm welcome, but it drew no response. The transporters left with some haste. Helen and a female security guard led the client, whose name was Amelia, back to her secured bedroom. Unlike Rinai's, it would never be left unlocked when Amelia was left alone there. She was thus, in effect, a client/prisoner, but this was in keeping with the range of services offered.

"Looks like a heavy case," Bart said as we watched. "Likely to impact our home life."

"We'll give you an easy out-patient to balance things off."

"Oh? What did you have in mind?"

"A high state official with shoplifting problems."

"You've got to be kidding."

"Afraid not. Like you say, we have to raise some cash cows to stay in business."

"I don't think I quite put it that way."

I got along with Bart reasonably well, but I sometimes sensed resentment in him towards me in particular. It could only have been my position as assistant director. He apparently saw me as less suitable for the job than himself, so it galled him to work under my authority. The fact was, however, that Dr. Gruner was so determined to hire Helen, enthralled by her combination of intelligence and compassion, that he was willing to employ her husband just to seal the deal. If not for his wife, Bart would not even be working at the Center.

Although, it must be said, I was beginning to have some doubts about the Center itself.

Partly to reassure myself, to gain a sense of solid goals and progress, I had Rachel meet with me in Dr. Gruner's office to discuss Rinai. We sat at the work table, the vacant director's chair an imprimatur for my advice and decisions.

"The night matron working out okay?" I asked.

"For me, great. The all-nighters were starting to pile on. More normal for Rinai, too."

"Yes, sorry about the delay." I refrained from blaming Dr. Gruner. "I suppose you've gained some initial impressions by now."

"Well, she doesn't seem especially needy. She's outwardly phlegmatic. Doesn't express any interests, though she'll page through magazines, likes the pictures. I have to initiate and direct all conversations. She only gives brief responses, very short comments. Rather blunt and yet often evasive."

"Evasive about what?"

Rachel looked up as she collected her thoughts. She was the youngest of our group, athletic and quite attractive, with a mop of black curls and olive complexion. She favored golden hoop earrings, or others that hung down.

"Well, take family. She'll rattle off some names, difficult, unpronounceable unless you know the language. But when I ask about mother, father, sister, brother, she'll look away as if they're esoteric concepts. It's as if she, and others I suppose, circulate or are passed around in some sort of fluid social matrix."

"Anything about religion or something like it?"

"Just a muddier version of what was in your notes. The idea of sacrifice based on fear of some terrible being, the common primitive pattern. She didn't get into so many details, though, like she did with John."

"Yes, he was really gaining insights with her. Of course, he'd gained access through Sven, had that advantage."

"Oh, but there was something I noticed. One night, entirely by accident. It was late, I'd slept a little already. I happened to pass her room, thought I should peek in and check on her, not sure why, just a feeling. She wasn't in bed. She was on the floor on the side away from me, squatting before something glowing orange in the darkness. And there was a smell, a scent, coarse like weeds or wildflowers, something like pepper or sharp spice. Rinai had her back to me so I couldn't see what it was."

"What did you do?"

"I closed the door as quietly as I could. Whatever was going on, something told me I shouldn't butt in. I guess that conflicts with the first feeling I had, but things seemed under control and I didn't have a good response ready. Anyway, I stayed awake a long time in case something happened. The next day, Rinai was just the same as usual."

"Well, you did the right thing, Rachel."

"Should we alert the night matron?"

"No, I don't think so. She's basically on-call for the residents. And there's security guards nearby."

"Do you have any idea what she was doing?"

"No, not really. Some cultural fetish, perhaps." I paused a moment, shifting in my chair. "But Rachel, I have to let you know. This could become a very challenging case with time—more challenging, I mean, than the others we're taking in, extreme though they are and higher profile. We might meet with things that our training and experience have not prepared us for. If you ever feel threatened and want to pull back, it's okay. I could step in and take full responsibility for the work. You could get an alternate assignment then, or perhaps you could stay and assist. It's a very special case that way, needs everything we can give it."

"No, I want to stay with it. I want to be the lead worker."

I looked at her fully, her resolve, her youth. I thought of John.

"Of course," I smiled. "I'm sure you'll be fine."

I'd said all I could, I thought, to warn her. I couldn't expect her–or anyone–to share in my speculations, which were, after all, influenced by past experiences, other places and times, technically unrelated. I was also influenced, I knew, by my desire to be the most direct worker, rather than mentor or supervisor, on a case that dealt with purest evil.

❦

Working alone in my office, I finalized the assignment of the shoplifting state official to Bart. I put in calls to the official's lawyer and the state inspector general to let them know. Feeling confident from this achievement, I checked my incoming emails for other pending matters. I was immediately drawn to a message from Dr. Gruner.

"Delayed in the Caribbean," it read, "with a special donor. Snake-youth being shipped there overland. Airlines wouldn't accept. Hired worker Rudy Twinkler for the case. He should be there before client. Alert security."

I had mixed feelings about this. The case would no doubt bring in hefty fees, good for the Center's finances. Also, its sensational aspects would be good for publicity. On the other hand, I wasn't sure we could manage such a volatile client. Piling on security guards only took us so far. The second-to-second possibility of attack was not good for building rapport and gaining insights. This Rudy Twinkler was apparently John's replacement, so I hoped Dr. Gruner's judgment had not been impeded in his current overwrought state.

Uneasy, I got up and walked to my window, tall and narrow, looking out on snowy knolls and a mixture of evergreens and bare-branched trees. For all their severity, I thought, none of these incoming cases approached Rinai's in subtlety and deviousness of causality. Clinical conundrums, yes, but basically just exaggerations of pedestrian issues. Rinai's case was unique, yet universal in its importance, rooted in the ancient perils to humankind. Not that such evils could be defeated, but once well known they could be managed. And most important to me, of course, they distracted from banality, the pathetic soap operas of life.

⊜⊶⊰⊱⊷⊜

"I really didn't think you were serious," Midori said.

"Oh, I'm almost always serious, more or less."

"Lot of wiggle room there."

She was skillfully dissecting her filet, even halving the mushrooms. Around us was velvety ambience, candlelight, others in retreat from their work between the holidays.

"When's this Twinkle guy coming?" she asked.

"It's Twinkler, and I don't exactly know. Supposed to be before his client. If he doesn't show, we're in the jail business."

I returned to my sole, giving a strong squeeze to the lemon wedge.

"He expects a lot from you, doesn't he?"

"Gruner? Yes, I suppose he does."

"Frees him up, I guess, for other ventures."

"What, you mean outside the Center?"

"Way outside. You don't think it's all about fund-raising, do you?"

I reflected a moment.

"He does seem pretty cozy there in the Caribbean. A break from us and the family, too."

"He's got that reputation. I heard about it when I was making the move."

47

"Yet still you came."

"I move around a lot. I need to. It's my destiny."

"Destiny?" I smiled.

"Not so scientific, eh? Well, not everything is. Outside the box, outside the matrix, outside the helix."

"Sounds a bit perverse."

"Just as you like, right? I'm for the loo."

She slipped out of the booth and stepped off briskly. Watching her go, her petite form blending with shadows and soft colors, I wondered if I'd underestimated her. There can be facets to a complex person that are not readily visible. When Midori returned, I noticed a certain grace about her that had escaped me before. In a relaxed state, she was quite attractive to me.

"I saved your steak from the waiter."

"Thank you."

I myself had finished but continued nibbling bread with my wine.

"Will you need a DNA test on snake-boy?" she asked.

"I'm sure there'll be one in the records."

"Gruner might not trust it."

"Wait until he asks for it. The client is dangerous. Don't try to take blood. Use his hair or saliva."

"Oh," she looked up coyly, "you care about me."

"Damn right I do."

She finished and sat back with satisfaction.

"Shall we split a dessert?"

While we sat waiting for it, an idea occurred to me.

"You know, speaking of DNA tests, I could use one on Rinai. I think she'll be very cooperative. She has been so far."

"Sure, no problem."

"Only keep the results confidential, secret in fact. And don't even tell anyone the type of test you're doing."

Rudy Twinkler had not yet arrived by New Year's. I'd planned to take the day off, but I stopped by the Center to check on things. I felt uneasy being away with Dr. Gruner gone, with pending new arrivals who had no dates or times. I found our phalanx of security guards—six now—looking bored but well distributed around the building. We now merited a sergeant, white shirt instead of khaki, who greeted me deferentially.

"Afternoon, sir. All quiet, everything in order."

I found Helen working with Amelia, trying to improve communication through the haze of medications. It was a slow process, difficult, requiring the full concentration of Helen's benign energies. This left Rinai mostly on her own, something I wasn't entirely comfortable with. I spotted her in the small gym, bouncing a volleyball off the wall.

"Getting enough sleep, Rinai?"

She gave a slight smile.

"How's the food? Getting enough to eat?"

"It's all artificial."

"Well, maybe we can do something about that. Do you like the people here?"

"Rachel is good. Too many police. I miss the old place."

"The farm in Scania? With Sven?"

She looked puzzled a moment, then: "There was sacrifice."

She resumed bouncing the ball off the wall. I'd said a bit too much, I thought, and yet I persisted.

"Do you miss your mother, your talks with her, her advice to you?"

The puzzlement again.

"My mother?"

She showed a bemused smile, then slammed the volleyball

49

hard off the wall and let it bounce away. She turned from me and walked to a corner of the gym, where she sat and sulked.

"See you later," I waved, and walked out as casually as I could.

As I passed Amelia's room, I asked Helen to check on Rinai later, calm her down as best she could. Continuing through the building, I was conscious of a tension in the air, a charged atmosphere to which I myself contributed. It was almost palpable, an expectation of not something I wanted but what I knew was unavoidable, inevitable given the nature of the Center and my own need to discover a certain Source, the ultimate depth from which came the darkest deeds and imaginings of our supposedly civilized world.

I reached my office door and found it unlocked. I was positive I'd locked it when last I'd left.

I entered.

Standing in the middle of the room, I detected a faint odor of vegetation, similar to the one in the restroom on the plane, but less pungent. I also noticed that my desk chair was partly pulled out and askew, rather than pushed in against the edge of the desk as I always left it. I strolled a bit around the room. There was something different about the bookshelf. I normally kept the two largest books first and last in the row, just inside the two bookends, black iron eagles. Now one of the large books, a dictionary, was third in the succession. In addition, a narrower book toward the middle of the row was not properly pushed in. It was *The Modern Guide to Necromancy*, by Funk. I saw no bookmark or notations. The articles on my desk were pretty much as I'd left them, I thought, the contents of the wastebasket an uninformative jumble.

I locked the office as I left, seeing no damage or marks on the hardware. There was not enough cause to involve the security guards, I judged. Not yet, anyway.

I was relaxing with a drink that evening when I got a call from Security Sgt. Hendon, who was working a staggered shift at the Center. He informed me that snake-boy had arrived, the crew of a long-distance ambulance waiting for him to be admitted so they could leave. Helen and the psychiatric nurse had left. Only the night matron remained to service the clients.

"What's the client's condition?" I asked.

"Woozy. Coming off sedation. Won't be no problem for a while."

"See if they can dose him again. Either way, put him in one of the no-window rooms, locked in till morning. We'll pick up on it then. Warn the matron to stay away."

I continued sipping my drink, imagined the scene at the Center. Dr. Gruner might have rushed off to attend to it personally, but I was only standing in for him and had not created the situation. He had. The new work day would be challenging enough without tackling it on a bad night's sleep. The new support staff would have to be greeted and oriented, as well as Rudy Twinkler if he could be located.

I made no effort to be early, a rebellious streak stirring within me. I therefore found eight people waiting for me in the lobby under the scrutiny of two security guards. The guards had also deposited two individuals in my office, a new client accompanied by a hospital social worker. The client was a tall and strong-looking young man, a non-verbal African immigrant who continually held his right arm extended straight out in front of him. An obvious psychosomatic case.

"This is all we have on him," the worker said, handing me a thin folder, "and here's the approved referral faxed to us by Dr. Gruner."

I glanced at the papers, saw they'd gotten the client from the Travelers' Aid Society. Someone had apparently dumped him at a bus station. The worker got up to leave. He seemed irritable, maybe because I'd come in late, he having to wait an extended time with the unpredictable client. I saw no way or reason to detain him so he was quickly out the door.

"What is your name?" I asked the young man.

His eyes shifted to me briefly but otherwise no response. He simply sat rigidly in his chair, arm held out ceaselessly, showing no fatigue whatever.

"Do you know where you are?"

Again no response.

"Do you speak English?"

Nothing.

"Hablas español? Tu parlez français?"

He remained mute, eyes forward.

As I considered what to do next, I noticed a message pinned under the phone to my right. It had been written by one of the night security guards. Rudy Twinkler had been detained at the airport for possession of a controlled substance. He required intervention by the Center to gain his release. I settled back in my chair and let this sink in, considered it in light of the snake-boy being locked in a windowless room elsewhere in the building. Clearly, the calls for immediate action were piling up. It was time for me to jettison some responsibility. I phoned the office shared by the Dudleys.

"Bart, please come to my office. And bring the psychiatric nurse if she's available."

They arrived as I was printing the email in which Dr. Gruner assigned Rudy Twinkler. I handed it to Bart along with the message from night security. He mumbled some irritation, but the assignment was well within the scope of his duties. Of course, I could understand his dislike of starting the work year having to rescue his supposed equal from a peccadillo.

"This may involve some expense," he said.

I handed him the Center's credit card left by Dr. Gruner.

"It'll work at the ATM. Just drop it off when you return."

The psychiatric nurse, whose name was Lucia, had been

apprehensively assessing the young man with arm extended. With Bart gone, I turned to putting her at ease so the client could be moved along. I still had the eight new staff to deal with.

"We won't be doing anything with him for a while," I said. "I'll get a worker assigned, maybe one of the new people, but Dr. Gruner will have to analyze him. Just get him secure in a room for today. I'll get a guard to accompany you."

"Nobody knows how he got this way?"

"It's a complete mystery. But there's extreme dysfunction, so here he is."

I was hoping, with this and other clients, that I did not sound glib in discussing them. The problem was, with my intense interest in pure evil and its sources, the lesser vicissitudes of human experience were of correspondingly less interest to me.

⊕⊬₿⊸⊁⊹⊱⊷⊶

The eight new workers were in Dr. Gruner's office, filling out various forms. I'd left them there after doing the traditional meet-and-greet, each of them delivering a rosy biography and show of enthusiasm. It was a good time-killer, giving me a chance to relax, moving the morning along toward lunch. There were three kitchen staff, three secretaries, and two case aides. I'd be placing them in their work stations after the paperwork. For now, though, I roamed the building, looking for reasons to believe all was well, stopping at windows to view a light snowfall on evergreens and dormant lawns. On one such stop I happened to sight two figures in the distance, walking slowly together and talking. As I continued watching, I came to realize they were Rinai and Rachel, looking entirely natural in each other's company, almost sisterly. It appeared to me that rapport had been achieved, which was good, though this was only my intellectual judgment. It was tinged with another, competing reaction, entirely emotional: envy. Thoughts of my failure with Rinai in the gym couldn't be kept from coming to mind.

Continuing through the building, I discovered that the client with extended arm had been installed in a windowless room. This vaguely bothered me. I could understand how the nurse and guard could be thinking of safety, maximum security for a large, seriously disturbed young man. But without stimulation, at least a window to the world, whatever wound had crippled the young man's psyche would fester and increase its dominance. He would clearly have to be moved, I decided.

⊕⊷⊰⊱⊹⊱⊰⊷⊕

"So when are you going to give me a case?" Midori asked.

We were in bed in my apartment, our first dinner having suggested a reprise, this time with added intimacy.

"God," I answered, "can't we ever get away from work?"

"No. Which is why we do it."

I took a moment to sort this out.

"So it's true for you too, eh?"

"People will be wondering," she went on, "especially if they find out about this."

"This?"

"Us!"

"Yes, yes. I see. Well, this last one I thought the male aide could handle. Lyle. Rather simple, actually, could be in a regular state hospital. You'd just be wasted on it. And I need you to be available on Rinai. That case is our main priority, the *only* one as far as I'm concerned."

"You mean, among the cases."

I laughed.

"Of course. What I could do is, I could have Megan, the other aide, report to you for mentoring to pick up some lab and research skills."

"So then two of us would be working on zero cases."

"Oh, I'm sure there'll be stuff coming up. Don't worry, I'll take care of you all right."

She raised herself on one arm, moonlight glistening on her shoulder. Her tousled waves of hair cast a shadow over my face, which she nonetheless scrutinized.

"Your personal assistant, then? Sort of a gofer?"

"Not at all. A partner in seeking new truths. In discovery. With obeisance to Dr. Gruner, of course."

"Oh, yes. Our founder and leader, wherever he may be."

Her voice trailed off dismissively as she came forward to kiss me, cover me with her body. I felt gratitude toward her, as I had with Astrid, but with Midori the comfort was more poignant, more timely. The burgeoning situation at the Center, Dr. Gruner's elusiveness and distant manipulations, my growing sense of reality as a slippery commodity, all combined to require some balance to the role I'd undertaken. The nearness and movements of Midori, the losing of my thoughts as I absorbed her passion, allowed the professional shell to dissolve and the true, ruthless hunter in me to challenge my evil prey. I was emboldened. Midori knew this and she also wanted it. A blinding crimson curtain enveloped us, no consciousness outside it. Then, for a while, simply no consciousness.

"The phone is ringing," came her voice from afar.

"Answer it," I struggled to respond.

I heard her soft hello, then she was back shaking me.

"It's a security guard from the Center. You have to talk to him. Something's happened."

I took the cordless handset from her. The tense voice of the guard, with confused noises in the background, began bluntly informing me of a horrific discovery behind the residential rooms of the Center. A female guard had exited the building to smoke a cigarette and, when she hadn't returned timely, another guard went to search for her. He found the woman lying on her back in the snow, stark in the light from one of the residential windows. The front of her torso and face had been severely damaged by a blast of some sort. To all appearances she'd been killed instantly, her remains left undisturbed thereafter. The local police had been called and were on-site, including a detective and soon a forensics person.

"Are any of our therapists there?"

"Yes, sir. Mr. Twinkler. Should I get him?"

"No, never mind. I'm on my way."

As I dressed, I let Midori know what had happened. She said that she'd come with me.

"Police forensics are involved," I said. "We can just get their report later."

"No, I want to be there myself."

She dressed incredibly quickly and was ready when I was. We were mostly silent in the car, both of us mindful of the natures of our clients and that of the Center and how it would all fit in a narrative about a bizarre horror. I was more privy, of course, to the details on Rinai, but I saw now that I must fully inform Midori.

"I'm glad you're coming along," I told her.

"I know you are."

IV.

"Bad it got into the news," said Dr. Gruner, planted again behind his desk.

"I talked with them about keeping it out, but they said no-can-do with a homicide."

"A rather quick determination, that."

"Well, there were no fragments from an explosion. Even her gun was still in its holster."

He sighed heavily.

"I got those financial commitments just under the wire. Fortunately. But we have to hold off on residential clients until after the investigation. We'll have to take those outpatient addiction cases. Did you look them over?"

"Yes," I answered, recalling his disdain for the type of client. "The two substance abusers I'd give to Helen and Bart. They could maybe do a group with Bart's shoplifter. The Internet freak I'd assign to Midori. Might be a help to her training her aide."

"Good thinking," the doctor nodded. "Done."

He was deeply tanned from his excursions and had gained a little weight. He'd also acquired what seemed an air if insouciance that was at odds with what I'd considered his professional focus. This did not bode well for the Center. His had been the vision at the heart of its raison d'être. My own inspiration had been mostly personal, opportunistic. I was assistant director only because he'd found me the most interesting among those he'd decided to hire. Thus, he'd be most comfortable discussing things with me. Unfortunately, I was not always as comfortable, could not always be candid.

"What about our initial client?" he asked me. "Any progress?"

"Some," I replied. "Rachel has done a good job establishing rapport with her, drawing out snatches about her past. They've taken walks together, gone on a shopping trip. Of course, Rinai is still fixated on the trauma at the farm, the events in Scania. As that's displaced by her experiences here, I expect we'll hear more about her earlier life."

"That would be good, I'd say necessary. Any way it can be facilitated, perhaps accelerated, we should undertake."

"Yes, doctor. Actually, I've asked Dr. Tateyama to do a DNA analysis."

His eyes widened.

"DNA? What made you think of that?"

"She had to do one on the snake client, so I asked her to test Rinai concurrently. Cover every possibility. I didn't think it could hurt."

"No, I suppose not. Well, let me know the results when you have them."

Later, with Gruner immersed in other matters, I went to see Midori in the lab. Megan was with her, so we talked out in the hallway.

"Actually, the test on Rinai is about finished. Nothing unusual. I was keeping the results to compare with snake-boy's. He showed an anomaly."

"Is he human?"

"Of course! But he has a partial deleted chromosome. I'm researching how it might cause his behavior."

"And nothing like that with Rinai," I thought out loud.

"No. You're back to cultural factors with her, and individual differences. No easy answers. Oh, but there was a call from the college lab, that little tusk we sent down."

"They found something more?"

"Could be. They tried an enhanced DNA analysis for very old material. This stuff was degraded more than they expected, so the animal was even more ancient than the extinct subspecies they had in mind. They believe it was a common ancestor to the later extinct animal and the modern babirusa."

"How many years back are we talking?"

"Think seven figures."

"And humans have been around–?"

"A million to two. Depending on your concept of human."

I thought for a moment, imagining the tusk.

"There was a hole drilled in the thing, for threading a cord or something through. The surface of the cut, if memory serves, seemed to match the outer surface."

"Yes, suggesting the driller was contemporaneous with the animal. Though someone in a later time could have found the tusk, cut the hole, and also worked on the surface."

"I suppose. But it might have been passed along continuously, assigned some special purpose. Perhaps a symbol of power."

"For a million years?"

"Okay, it's a stretch. But can you have them send it back here? We can maybe show it to Rinai, get her reaction."

"They're supposed to return it anyway, but I'll give them a call and hustle it along."

⊕⊢∃⊹⊱⊱⊢⊕

Passing by the gym, I noticed Rudy and one of the guards watching something out on the floor. They were smiling, the guard with his hand over his mouth. I moved closer for a better look. The snake-boy was wriggling swiftly across the polished tiles, inspecting a wide scattering of cream-filled snack cakes, apparently a therapeutic exercise devised by Rudy. He'd somehow gained favor with Dr. Gruner as an expert in CST, cross-species transference, an exotic California invention. Its application in the cream cake pursuit was beyond me, being of little interest beyond amusement, an attitude shared by the guard, I supposed, and maybe Rudy himself if the full truth were known. He was slightly overweight with longish sandy hair and matching moustache with goatee. He wore aviator glasses, tinted rose, and would look natural as a used yacht salesman.

Bart was coming down the hallway, stopped by the doors to the gym where I stood. I nodded a greeting. He gazed past me at the ongoing spectacle, frowning quizzically.

"What's going on?"

"A sort of therapy, I presume. By our new colleague."

"Hm."

My last word likely rankled him. The airport experience with Rudy had no doubt left an impression.

"So what do you think of this?" he asked.

I shrugged.

"He's Dr. Gruner's hire. Unilateral. We therefore have to work with him."

Bart was silent. I thought perhaps I'd been too blunt with him. I wasn't still running the place, after all.

"How's it going with your client?" I proffered.

"You know, I'm starting to think he's a phony. That this supposed shoplifting urge is all a ruse."

"Oh? Why would he do that? A high state official."

"I don't know. But it's there in his body language, the rehearsed tone, the practiced eye contact. He's looking to come out ahead somehow. Not here, of course, but somewhere."

"Maybe he's reaching out. Like the class clown in school.

He doesn't really want to be funny, not deep down. He wants someone to notice his need, help him with a more serious problem."

"Well, not necessarily. Some people just enjoy clowning. Or attention for its own sake."

As if on cue, Rudy burst out laughing in the gym. Bart and I peered in at him.

"He should really get an outside attorney for his next hearing," Bart proclaimed, "take some responsibility. It isn't the Center's mess just because it's his."

He was right, I thought, but with a caveat. The Center might be headed toward its own mess or messes so, before long, all available hands might be needed for our survival. Even Rudy's, clown or no. So we didn't want to fire ir disgruntle anyone, including Bart himself. A balance between conflicting demands was needed that I wasn't sure Dr. Gruner could achieve, especially in the shadows of devilry and homicide.

We sat before the computer screen in the dimly lit lab, Midori bringing up pages from the provisional forensics report.

"No accelerant could be found," she summarized, "burns extreme but death more likely from shock, position of body suggesting blast from close to building."

"But not from within it?"

"As far as we know, the clients' windows were closed."

"And the roof?"

"The angle wouldn't be right, assuming the guard was standing."

She brought up a photo of the wall and two windows, an X superimposed on the snow in the foreground.

"This is my own. As you can see, the body was between Rinai's and Amelia's windows, a little ways out. The X is slanted toward Rinai's because the legs were a bit in her direction. The light by which the body was found, however, came from Amelia's window."

"So the police questioned her."

"Yes. She had no explanation for what had happened, only said she heard a noise, turned on the light because she was afraid."

"And nothing from Rinai, of course."

"Almost mute, like she didn't know what they were talking about."

"Yes, I'm familiar with that."

"I looked around in the snow later but it was pretty well trampled. There was one thing, though. In the snow close to the building, there was some glazing on a patch next to Rinai's window. Not in front of it like you might expect. An outside heat source had singed the surface of the new snow, which quickly re-froze. There were no drips or fragments of any kind, and no footprints there. The police would have noticed those, of course."

"Did you tell them about the glazing?"

"No. I thought it would be of more use to you."

"Without their interference, you mean?"

"Yes."

I draped an arm over the back of Midori's chair, gazed with her at the image now on the screen, a rough oval superimposed on the snow next to Rinai's window.

"This could get rather spooky. Are you game?"

"As game as you are."

"How about for dinner?"

"Sure. But first I have these urine drops to do. The new addiction cases. And Rudy, by Gruner's orders."

"Okay. I'll take a walk."

〜❦〜

Passing the rear of the building, I stopped momentarily to inspect the crime scene. Recent snowfall had obscured whatever traces remained of the violence. Rinai's blinds were closed, Amelia's slightly open but no light issued. The sky was darkening with the onset of evening. I continued on along an indentation in the snow that was the submerged walkway. The maintenance contractor had failed to clear it, earning a demerit in my mental file. Some distance ahead, a coyote crossed my path with an extra-large rat in its mouth.

Much different than the East Indies, I thought, yet the evil Rinai brought adapts to our frozen culture as smoothly as when it killed John. Its origin, or at least its present source, has to be made known to gain control for rationality, to give it meaning and status as an antidote for terror. Without control, rationality is an impotent construct, all the good works in its name mere illusions. Evil then overlays the world in countless manifestations.

I came to the edge of the grounds, our border with recently built ranch homes. Their construction had coincided with the closing of the girls' detention facility. Its site was re-zoned for medical services, numerous evergreens planted to offset the gloomy deciduous trees, the cyclone fence removed though its postholes were still detectable. I followed their telltale markings to an unused shed on a corner of our grounds, just before a side street that intersected farther along with the street fronting the Center. I found the shed unlocked, the locking mechanism broken. I entered.

Pocket flasks of vodka and bottles of cheap wine had been consumed here, I saw, along with many cigarettes and an assortment of shiny-wrapped junk food. There were also small animal droppings but thankfully none human. Something was stuck on one wall that I needed my penlight to inspect, then wished I hadn't. A religious leaflet with an unwrapped condom in front of it had been skewered with a hypodermic needle. This last finding gave me pause, exceeding as it did the more mundane trappings of vagrancy. While the degenerate lifestyle is a true bane for civilization, albeit ever present, the attempt to make it a practiced art, assert it as identity, is an assault on rationality. It infuriated me, yet I found it fascinating, as I did the deeper circles of evil from which it sprang and which it served.

I exited the shed, strode to the side street close by. A man walking his dog approached the point on the sidewalk where I stood. He was short and stocky, middle-aged, vacant of expression. The dog was dark and lean, his eyes betraying an impulse I well recognized: the drive to hate and kill at the least provocation. I tensed my right leg for a high kick into the arc of his leap, my fingers closing on the pepper spray canister in my coat pocket.

"You're from that place over there," the man said, "aren't you?"

"Yes," I replied.

"You're the boss, the head guy."

"No. I work there, but I'm not the boss."

"They showed you talking to the cops on TV, like you was in charge. There was that murder."

"Yes, but I'm not in charge there. The director was away, so the cops talked to me instead."

The man looked toward the Center as he digested this, his companion tugging on his leash in my direction.

"The other day," the man resumed, "I saw a couple guys in there, one walking like Frankenstein. The other guy was leading him around, trying to get him to hug trees, it looked like. Showing him how."

"I can't talk about the patients."

"Yeah, well, the one guy looked dangerous."

I remained silent. The dog shifted about restlessly.

"You ever have a dog?" the man asked.

"Yes, but he had to be put down."

"Aw, that's a shame. Why?"

"He tried to kill someone."

"Oh. Yeah, that's bad. But you gotta train 'em right. Barnaby here I was real strict with. You could trust him now with a fresh cooked pot roast, just him and it in the room."

The dog was again alert upon hearing his name, knew he was being praised, gave a low growl at my doubtful look. His master didn't seem to notice.

"Well, I have to be getting back," I said. "I don't want to get fired. Nice meeting you, sir. Goodbye, Barnaby."

The dog momentarily looked surprised, then eyeballed me sourly as I moved away. Perhaps he sensed the declining respect I felt toward dogs in general. I was coming to believe they were overrated, along with all other pets. For companionship, protection, or whatever purpose, they were mediocre substitutes for better means. Parasites, basically. With middle-aged to elderly people, especially, the solicitous treatment they received was like the attention typically given a child.

"Have a good walk?" Midori asked on my return.

"Couldn't have been better," I responded.

❄❀❄

On talking with Lyle, the male aide in charge of our extended-arm client, I discovered it was not he who'd been giving the client tree hugging lessons. It had been Rudy Twinkler. I found this presumptuous on Rudy's part and was irritated, but I hesitated to confront him since Dr. Gruner seemed to favor him. The best I could do was try to influence the director about setting limits.

"I know we emphasized flexibility," I said to him, "but that was to be in response to our expectations, our assignments. Here we seem to have a worker responding more to his own priorities, setting his own agenda."

Dr. Gruner folded his hands, looking concerned. It was rare that we didn't readily agree.

"If he pulled rank on the aide, that was wrong," the director intoned. "The assigned worker winds up accountable for the case. But, at this point, perhaps the best solution is simply to make Rudy the worker, Lyle staying on as his aide."

"Shouldn't we see how he does with his first case, the snake persona, before giving him another one?"

"Oh, I have full confidence in him on that. He's an expert in CST, he's enthusiastic. I'm sure he has it well in hand and can take on something else."

"Who did you say recommended him to you?"

"A lady who is one of our most generous supporters."

"And how did she happen to know him?"

A hesitation, then: "She's his mother."

"Oh."

To change the subject, I returned to my encounter with the man and his dog, suggested there was a lack of understanding by the community regarding our function. It might help, I proffered, to designate a liaison of some sort, someone to reach out with information and assurance to mitigate our neighbors' fears.

"Who did you have in mind for this role?" Gruner asked.

"Helen would seem a logical choice."

The director nodded, considering.

"Of course, she already has two cases, as well as backing up Rachel on Rinai."

"Her addiction case could go to Bart, since he has another substance abuser already and they're in a group. His shoplifter could go to Lyle, since Bart thinks the case is bogus and is just going through the motions with it. Lyle's other case we've already moved to Rudy, right?"

Dr. Gruner sat back and stared, then smiled wryly.

"Take care of the announcements. It's nice to know we have everything under control."

On leaving the director's office, I realized that my trust in his leadership was declining. While he respected the importance of Rinai's case, my lead involvement in it, he seemed to be easily compromised in most other matters at the Center. Excessively absent, making cavalier decisions, giving someone like Rudy free rein, he would eventually turn the Center into another community boondoggle, long on self-praise but just empty, suffocating fluff to most serious professionals. It would then be useless in the vital, compelling quest I was now engaged in, the search for a primary source of evil, perhaps the worst on earth, with roots grown deep into regions not heretofore accessed, though imagined by some in their darkest speculations.

⊕ӊↈↈↈↈ

The lead secretary informed me that I had an international call. I immediately thought of Astrid, that we were overdue for a phone contact, that it was strange she was calling me at the office instead of at the apartment. I had the secretary put the call through.

It was Nils Sjoberg, Astrid's senior partner.

"We captured the suspect in your colleague's murder," he informed me.

"Oh? I thought he'd left the country."

"As did we. But he had second thoughts about crossing the ice, tried to wait for it to thicken. He hid in a shed, stole food, got caught when he built a fire for warmth. Our bulletin was all around by then, even Finn-side."

"Well, that's great. I'm glad you got him."

"Yes. Of course, there's the prosecution now to deal with. I'm afraid they'll need you to testify, being the only witness to the crime. The hearing is set for Thursday next week. There could maybe be a continuance if that's too soon for you. Your consulate here says they can help with your arrangements."

It was apparently presumed that I would want to make the trip. But that was understandable, I quickly realized, and right. This was about John, his vicious murder.

"Never mind the continuance," I told Nils. "I'll be there next week."

When we'd finished with the details and hung up, I reflected on my eagerness to go. Perhaps the situation at the Center fed into it, as well, of course, as my continuing attraction to Astrid. When last we'd parted, there was no question it was what both of us needed to do. If that were true, however, I'd be reluctant to travel now, so far and so suddenly, from the working site of my mission. Even the prospect of seeing Astrid would not cause me to drop everything. Yet it now seemed eminently doable, with the added twist of giving Dr. Gruner a taste of his own medicine.

Late in the day, mulling the handling of Rinai's case in my absence, I went to the lab to see Midori. She was privy now to the facts and possibilities involved, so it was logical she should work with Rachel and be my eyes and ears, so to speak. I found her examining a specimen with Megan, explaining something apparently complex. Then I saw it was the eons-old babirusa tusk. My added knowledge of it caused it to hold my gaze a moment, during which the two women noticed me.

"May we help you?" Midori smiled.

"I see the college returned our evidence."

"Just came a little while ago. They said it belongs in the natural history museum when we're done with it."

"That won't be for a while yet." Then, to Megan: "I take it you know all about it now."

"Just the physical properties, the age. It's a very interesting artifact."

"Yes. Midori, I need to talk with you later about something for next week. Right now, I'd like to borrow our little charm here for a session with Rinai. Just a short one."

Midori registered my meaning.

"Were you planning to do it alone? Rachel's left for the day. Want me to come along?"

I hesitated, imagined Rinai's negative reaction to me, didn't want it spilling over to Midori.

"Actually, it might work best if I took Megan. I'll explain it all later."

Midori stared a moment, then shrugged, bemused by my apparent caprice.

"Can you do overtime?" she asked her protégé.

"Of course!" came the eager reply.

Walking the hall with Megan, I briefly envied her innocence. She was very young, light brown hair casually tied back, and showed anticipation far removed from the dread I felt myself. The object I carried might be mere ornamentation or a harmless talisman, or else a harmful one, the knowledge of which Rinai might share with John's murderer. There was the green powder, after all, the sacrifices at the farm, the bizarre stories from her homeland. Her reaction to the ancient tusk might well tie her to the person–the humanoid–now in custody at the detention facility in Scania.

We found her lounging in her room, perhaps waiting for dinner. She smiled at Megan as we entered but ignored myself. The women exchanged brief pleasantries. Rinai seemed to be in an accessible mood.

"We won't be long," I assured her.

I brought out the tusk, watched her eyes and mouth open more.

"Can you tell me what you know about this?"

She looked at me directly with an expression of wonder, then back at the tusk.

"It was Sven's," she replied.

"It belonged to Sven?"

"Yes. He always had it."

"Where did he get it?"

"His family. A grandmother, great-mother. Someone."

I hesitated, wondered where to take this.

"Did you meet this relative?"

"No. She was dead, long time ago. Gave that to Sven when she died."

"Does it have some meaning?"

"Meaning–"

She looked off into space, her eyes vacant.

"Something it stands for, something it's used for."

"It was the cause of him seeking me, of our marriage."

"Please explain."

"The great-*grand*mother, I think it was, had knowledge of ancestors very, very far back. They lived in that part of the world I am from. But before that, much before that, a time lost in time, they began in the great cold continent to the south. Those first people are forgotten, all traces gone, but the ones great-grandmother knew lived very much like my own people. It is a way cut off from the world, the outside seen as hostile because it is different. I was raised in this life and so its ways are within me, and its beliefs, even its practices, its ceremonies."

She stopped, frowned as if trying to recall something.

"You were going to tell me how the tusk led Sven to seek you."

"Yes. Yes, I will tell you. There was something–a power– in the little horn, the power that drove Sven to find out about us, to seek a wife from us to end his solitude, a wife to restore his branch of the clan to the central source of its power. He had to do it, to ease the strong lacking he felt, that he always felt. It had to be, had to happen to give him true life in this world."

"So he went to the International Pen-Friend League, specified your country, its autonomous region, and your tribal group, the clan. Somehow, they matched you with him."

"There were several of us. The headman chose me. There was money paid."

"I see. Did you want to go with Sven?"

"There was no talk of wanting, no thought. The headman decided. It was sacrifice."

"Sacrifice to whom?"

"The Kakili." This in a whisper.

"I've heard that he controls monsters."

Rinai was silent, her expression wary.

"Did you like your new country?" Megan broke in.

Rinai relaxed, the question's apparent purpose.

"Yes," she smiled at my companion.

"There must have been many challenges."

"Sven was good. He helped me."

Megan nodded and looked over at me, yielding back. I still held the babirusa tusk.

"And, just to be clear, Rinai, Sven already had this before you met him? Before maybe he went to the Pen-Friend people?"

"Yes, from the great-grandmother."

"Did he already know about the sacrifices? The need for them?"

"Sven did sacrifices himself, his own will. It was secret, not for outsiders, but a living part of our life."

I ached to ask again about the Kakili, but I didn't want to blow the interview. It was a success as it stood, Rinai had opened up, and I had to leave the case in good shape for my absence.

"Well, thanks for talking with us, Rinai. We'd better let you get ready for dinner now."

She didn't disagree. Megan plied me with questions on our way back to the lab, but I minimized what I told her about the case. I didn't know her well yet.

❦

Midori drove me to the airport on the day of my departure, arriving quite early. We sat in the bar to await my boarding time. I had a double brandy, John's drink, while Midori nursed a glass of white wine.

"Getting an early start on business class?" she joked.

"Actually, they put me in coach."

"How did that happen? A mistake?"

"I don't know. The secretary gave the voucher to Gruner for his signature. He maybe had her change it."

"He's been kind of out of sorts the last few days. Pissed about your leaving, you think? Seems kind of low, a plane ticket."

"He's been different since that endowment tour. Something must have happened."

"Mrs. Twinkler, maybe? Rudy's mom?"

"No, he was fine with that. Got what he wanted. He got hung up down in the Caribbean, no clear return time, then had to hustle back when the guard was killed."

"And that's still unsolved."

"Yes. A disruption for him, lasting. Now I'm taking off on him. But I really have no choice, no good one anyway, and he should understand that, make the adjustment. He's a psychiatrist, after all."

"They're the worst at some things. Personal matters."

"That reputation you said he had. Think he might've had a mistress down there?"

"Hey, I'm just a working girl sipping wine."

And she did so. We sat in near-silence awhile, mulling our

imminent separation, but we'd been intimate too short a time to get emotional over it. There was also the plan for our work which took priority, her necessary involvement in Rinai's case during my absence. This was in fact why I liked Midori, her supportive nature, though I doubted she'd want to accompany me on the full course of my work against the Kakili.

Alone later in the boarding area, I reflected on how any one life amounts to very little by itself. All the wonders of civilization were accomplished over generations, sometimes centuries.

The evil attempts to disrupt or destroy this progress, however, tend to rise and fall within a single generation. Nevertheless, the attempts do occur, often cyclically, bearing stark similarities to atrocities long past. Anachronisms, primitive and yet inevitable. The evil surrounding Rinai, its unmitigated violence, suggested a source reaching out through her from her homeland, a specific point within it rooted to another and deeper source, timeless, the genesis itself of evil on earth. Intentional or not, Sven had facilitated its spread, cousin as he was to Rinai's clan.

Before Midori and I had left the bar, there was a news story on the television about a dog-fighting ring. It seemed lighter fare compared to the usual events reported: protracted wars with cloudy purposes, cascading crime in the cities, riots featuring anarchists and practiced looting, fragility of laws and leadership, irrational indifference to the crumbling of the planet and human life, debased religion and its ignorant, often vicious followers. This was what I was up against, I realized. And more. Forces like the Kakili were never satisfied. They consumed the night. They craved a steady diet.

"Good luck," Midori had said when we parted.

V.

I'd obtained an upgrade for the short second leg of my trip, so I was far more comfortable than I'd been over the ocean. It would also enable me to meet Astrid in a relaxed state. She was meeting me at the airport in Malmo and, the arrival time being late, we'd go directly to her apartment. We'd have wound up there also at an earlier hour, but we'd have stopped somewhere on the way. The end destination was predetermined by our prior collaboration and our love.

"You're back to being blonde," I said on seeing her.

"The roots were starting to show too much."

"But now you won't stand out in the crowd here."

"That's getting to be for the better."

She still had a vulnerable appearance, slender and very young, without aggressive mannerisms, but I'd learned by now of her inner strength. Without her, the transporting of Rinai would have been a greater and less rewarding task, and she seemed to be an effective officer there in Scania.

"Are you involved with the prosecution on John?" I asked as she drove.

"Nils has taken things over mostly. John's brother was putting on pressure through your consulate."

"Yes, he was miffed about getting information late. We couldn't locate him early on, or other family."

"Wasn't it in the papers or something over there?"

"Our director has connections, doesn't like bad news spreading."

I related his reaction to the killing of the guard, the fruitless investigation, the mystery surrounding Rinai. I told of showing her the ancient babirusa tusk.

"She claimed it was Sven's, entrusted to him by a great-grandmother. It apparently inspired him to reclaim an ancient heritage. Its basic elements, the customs and beliefs, are revered among Rinai's own people. Sven sought them out, bent on obtaining a bride who would link him to a source of unusual power, the culture of the Kakili. The power was diluted in his own lineage, dormant within him, but since genetically present it had potential for reclamation. Rinai then was a portal for Sven to superior existence, as he saw it, a predestined status in nature and the universe which had been usurped."

"Sounds pretty wild. Do you think your friend–your colleague, John–knew what was going on?"

"Maybe, but I don't know. He had a private talk with Rinai after Sven's killing. If he'd had any inkling, he would've persisted until he knew it all. That's how John was, and he was energized for it when he died."

"Maybe that's the reason he was killed."

"Could be, though it appeared spontaneous."

"But so have the other deaths, right? Appearances maybe deceiving, et cetera."

"Yes, that's true."

The streets seemed unusually quiet to me, but it was a weeknight and very late. The sky was moonless, starless. We arrived at Astrid's building and made our way to her apartment, several floors up. We barely spoke in deference to sleeping neighbors, this being a land of such deference, at least traditionally. Recent immigration had changed things in some places.

"Welcome back," she whispered as she unlocked the door.

Photosensitive nightlights provided a ghostly atmosphere in the apartment. They were all the light either of us needed or wanted, however, revealing well our route to the bedroom. Neither of us had mentioned the option of my staying in a hotel.

"Would you like anything?" she asked. "A drink or something?"

"Just you."

In the bedroom I sat upright in a club chair, my arms on the wooden ones of the chair, while Astrid changed in the bathroom. Her holstered gun, badge, and radio were on one end of a chest of drawers. As I viewed them I felt again the strain of my flight over the Atlantic, Dr. Gruner's pettiness in changing the ticket, his apparent indifference or ignorance toward the wider and greater issue I pursued. My irritation was assuaged, however, by the reappearance of Astrid. She wore a delicate peignoir, semi-transparent, that shifted as she walked and flattered her slim form within.

"Aren't you getting ready?" she asked.

"Give me ten seconds."

⊖⊣3⊰⊱⊱⊱⊱

The dawn next morning was late as usual, but it actually yielded some sunlight for a while. It gave the frost on the windows an etched-glass appearance. As we sat having breakfast, our relaxed absorption with each other gave way to confidence in the professional methods we shared. The world outside was manageable, we felt, and we could handle it, no matter how sinister its villains.

"You know," Astrid said, "you should probably talk to Sven's relatives. It seems you're taking Rinai's story at face value. The great-grandmother and all."

"You're right," I had to agree. "But didn't you talk with them yourself?"

"Our case had a different focus. Sven was strictly a victim. Now there's this tusk and Rinai's story. There's the relatives to test it against."

"And your own investigation is closed."

"Yes. The cases against Tapunui are with the district judge. Both killings, Sven and John."

"Not the farm hand we found?"

"Not yet. Later, I think, if he's convicted on Sven."

"Hm. I guess there's no interest here in Rinai."

"They didn't know what to do with her before. They were glad that you took her."

"Yes, along with something else, it seems. Two more killings worth."

We were both silent a moment.

"Look," Astrid said, "I can put you in touch with Sven's relatives, then I have to duck out."

"Sure, understood. But this suspect in the trial, do we know where he's from?"

"New Guinea or somewhere around it, according to our Indonesian official. That's going by the language. The subject himself is mostly uncooperative."

"And his name is what?"

"Tapunui. Translates to 'forbidden earth.'"

I parked the rental car in an attractive neighborhood near downtown and the theater district. There was an artist and student enclave nearby, so these types were prominent on the streets. Sven's uncle and aunt lived in a building of apartments more spacious than was typical of the city. The uncle, Frans, greeted me warmly, apparently appreciative of any interest in Sven and his demise. Tuva the aunt was more reserved. She wore her hair long for a middle-aged woman and wound in a braid, brown with streaks of gray.

"Coffee?" she asked crisply.

"Yes, thank you."

She went to get it while Frans ushered me to a chair. As I scanned the open floor plan, I was attracted by many cultural artifacts on the walls, shelves, tables, and displayed in glass cases. Many were weapons–spears, shields, swords, scimitars, bolos, krisses–along with ornate carved masks and headdresses, hand-painted and feathered. There were colorful embroidered wall hangings, jewelry strung with beads, shells, coins, small bones, and there were stuffed birds of paradise. The display extended throughout the apartment, a huge ceremonial drum the most distant object I could identify.

"I take it you're in the business," I proffered.

"Not at all. It's Tuva's hobby. Has been since we were married. I worked in a trucking company, retired now."

"Transportation?"

"Yes. Worked my way up to management. Different here than America, of course."

"Must have come in handy supplying this hobby."

He laughed.

"Well, not so often, actually."

"Do you ever run out of space?"

"No, she's quite disciplined that way. When overflow threatens, she moves out some things she can part with. Sells them on the Internet, mostly."

"How long has this been in progress?"

"We've been married 36 years."

Tuva returned with the coffee.

"We've been discussing your collection," her husband informed her.

She gave a polite smile and settled next to Frans on the couch, rather stiffly.

"I'm impressed," I said. "I'm familiar with some of the items, their workmanship. A few of the weapons, the masks, perhaps the jewelry. I've been to that part of the world, done some study of it."

Tuva eyed me warily.

"You were close to it?"

"Yes. I was not a tourist."

"How close were you?"

"I saw the variety in things, the details. For instance, the differences in bolos, their shapes and curvatures, the notches and decorations, symbols. Differences showing a weapon's origin in a particular tribe or subculture."

"So you are interested in weapons."

"Well, not so much for their being weapons. More for the culture and history behind them. Guns I find to be of much less interest, lacking the human connection, the spiritual story."

She nodded approvingly, Frans remaining mute.

"Yes," Tuva said, "they are dead things. No human strength behind them, just explosions. No intimacy, one to the other, in the taking of life. No risk in the closeness. Risk that one's fate may fall in any of many directions. The beauty of capitulation, acceptance."

She put one hand to her temple, half closed her eyes. I was suddenly reminded of Sven, his supposed obsession, and that I'd come here to discuss him.

"This is all so interesting, I hate to change the subject, but I have a question or two about Sven. Something I'd like to clear up. You see, after he died, an object was found in his house, a small tusk from an animal, very old, in fact ancient, prehistoric–"

"Do you have it with you?" Tuva interrupted.

"No. It's back in America, being tested."

"In America?"

"Yes."

She stared at me. I waited for her to speak, but instead she rose from the couch and left the room, no explanation to myself or Frans.

"We'll have to excuse her," he said. "She's become abrupt in recent years. It's simply her way now."

His statement had a practiced cadence, as if he'd repeated it many times in various situations. I could have inquired why, but I had my other direction to pursue. I simply told him I understood and continued as before.

"This object I mentioned, a sort of charm or talisman, was apparently given to him by a great-grandmother, your own maternal grandmother. Do you remember her?"

"Of course, but we never saw them much. They lived way up in timberland. He was an old merchant mariner. They met in a port on Sumatra."

"Do you recall her having this tusk that we think she gave Sven?"

"No, I never heard about it. Never saw it. Of course, that would be a very long time ago. She died while Sven was quite small."

"Do you know what she died of?"

"I think they just said old age, nothing more."

"And her husband, your grandfather?"

"He had some weird accident a short time later. Propane tank exploded. He was killed instantly."

I took a moment to absorb this, saw a pattern of some sort forming, a tapestry of coincidences. I looked to the nearby wall hangings and felt challenged by their boldness.

"As I said," Frans went on, "this was all a long time ago."

"Yes, of course."

I sat and listened as he drifted into banal but surprisingly personal topics: his and Tuva's meeting in business school, their inability to have children, her opposition to adopting. It was clear that Frans was isolated with this strange woman, controlled by her strangeness, their original attraction morphed into decadent symbiosis. Not uncommon, perhaps, but in this case suggesting the growth of subtler forms of the destructive force I pursued.

"Do you have much contact with Tuva's family?" I asked.

"She was a war orphan," Frans responded. "Her adoptive parents died rather young."

His wife had not returned and he did not call her for my departure. It was just as well, I thought. She'd seemed upset by something in our conversation and apparently had little contact with the outside world. Not unlike Rinai, it struck me. I thought about the couple meeting in business school and could easily picture Tuva as the manager of their relationship. How long had it taken her to be disappointed in Frans, his lack of strong interest in her "hobby?" But whatever his faults in her eyes, however deep his mediocrity, it might well have saved him from a fate resembling Sven's.

<hr/>

I decided to check in with Nils while Astrid was doing field work, thus respecting his role, more or less, as my primary contact with the Scania district police. He was to be my escort to the trial in the district court having jurisdiction. It was in the area where the crimes were committed, a day trip though not a short drive, Nils advising we'd be starting out at dawn.

"I'll be ready," I promised, delaying the revelation that I was staying with Astrid.

He brought out the files on crimes committed at the farm: three murders, arson on the chicken coop, breaking and entering, animal abuse, and possible violation of immigration law. There was also a slim file on the suspect, only charged for now with two of the murders.

"What's the penalty if he's found guilty?" I asked.

"Ten to eighteen years per murder, possibly less, and maybe served concurrently. Life imprisonment is also possible, but with foreigners there's an eye towards deportation, so the shorter sentence is preferred."

I thought for a moment of John, his life worth only a ten-year sentence in this country, perhaps only half that sentence. Nils read my thoughts.

"I'm not saying I agree with it," he said. "Nor does forty percent of the population. It's simply the society we have for now, though it could all be changing soon."

"I wish you well on that."

"Anyway, we'll do all we can to nail this bastard for the maximum."

"How does the evidence look?"

Nils sighed heavily.

"Mostly circumstantial except for your I.D. There were footprints his size in the mud, a machete with smudged prints thrown away, two tramps and a worker saw him hop the train, the worker he threatened. He didn't confess, wouldn't say anything at first, then he had to have a lawyer so that was that."

"What about on Sven's murder?"

"Very little. He was around, he's mean. Mostly window dressing for the charge regarding your friend."

"I see. And there's nothing in his background to connect him with either crime?"

Nils flipped open the thin file.

"What background?"

I saw the file copies of a Blue Notice sent through Interpol and letters sent to police agencies around New Guinea, along with their negative responses. There were also large photos of the suspect and recordings of his arrest and arraignment.

"I suppose he'll be cleaned up for the trial," I commented.

"It's a standard part of defense strategy."

I gazed at the shaggy, bearded visage before me, his hulking stance. There was latent hostility in the eyes, resentment, the subject seemingly oblivious to others' suffering, his depravity in causing it. He was a creature familiar to me, entirely without character and deserving of expungement.

"How close were you to him?" Nils asked.

I somehow hadn't realized that it might be an issue.

"Let's see. Sixty, seventy meters or so. Wasn't the distance measured by someone?"

"No. The local responders didn't properly mark the spot. With the rain and tramping about, we could only guess later. Round it down when they ask you, say sixty meters. And you had a nice clean window, right? The rain washing it off?"

"Well, I suppose so."

"Good. But be definite about it. You'll have the lay judges behind you, the local advisors to the presiding judge. They want this person far away from their community, sent across the world somewhere."

I glanced through the negative response letters, wondering which country might be the deportation host.

"Any chance he could be sent to America?"

"To be re-tried for your colleague's murder? No, afraid not. Besides our jurisdiction, we never extradite when capital punishment might be applied. Another issue here."

He was still speaking when something caught my eye on one of the response letters. Although the agency could not match an individual to the photos and fingerprints, they listed several entities suggested by the natures of the crimes committed. One was referred to as "cult of Kakili." I looked through the letters once more but found no further reference, just the one mention with no elaboration. I tried to display no reaction, seeing no point in re-involving Nils with Rinai at this point.

"So," he spoke to my distraction, "crack of dawn on trial day, right?"

"Oh, yes. Right."

"The lobby at your hotel?"

I hesitated a moment, recalling the reservation they'd made for me.

"Sure thing. I'll be ready."

I resolved to stop by the place and register on my way back to Astrid's apartment.

⊙⊷⊰❧⊱⊷⊙

We stayed in rather than dining out, Astrid preparing beef rydberg while I sipped a Romanian wine from her cabinet. I'd have preferred something stronger, but her company lessened the need for intoxicant, especially after the sessions with Sven's relatives and Nils. Relaxing in Astrid's living room, hearing the domestic sounds from her kitchen, I momentarily questioned my long-evolving preoccupation with evil. A necessary work, yes, I saw this, but as the focus of one's existence was it not quixotic in the end? It involved a struggle between great pervasive forces, amorphous in their forms, that had persisted through all known time. The comfort of a home, a spouse and family, on the other hand, could be known and accomplished within one's own lifetime. Eternal struggles could be seen and recognized without allowing them to dominate.

"I noticed you before," Astrid said over dinner, "like you were deep in thought."

"Obscure reflections," I responded, "futile in the end."

"What end?"

I stopped in mid-forklift.

"Got me there," I smiled at her. "I suppose there really isn't any, aside from the obvious one."

"No end to work, maybe? Your–our–specific work?"

"Yes. No end as there was no beginning. We just fall into things, it seems."

"Well, of course I was born in a police family. That mostly accounts for me, I think. With you, wasn't it that trip you took? The primitive culture? The cobra?"

I laid down my fork, distracted from the delicious meal and even from Astrid, mindful of a childhood when nourishment of any sort was scarce.

"No, it was earlier. I had several siblings. My father was sometimes out of work, my mother overwrought, had problems. I saw some kids better off, others from families like our own. A kid hit me with a brick once, his family laughed up on the porch. I saw cruelty to animals, didn't understand it. Children can be cruel, extremely so. It's the norm. They are not innocent. The fights at school and in the neighborhood, it wasn't just to win the fight, it was to cause pain and enjoy it. When someone was beaten he still got hit, or kicked. There were gangs. Dirty tricks were played on store owners, their windows messed up, dog droppings placed on the ledges underneath."

Astrid laid down her fork as well.

"So, these things decided–influenced–your direction in life?"

"Somewhat, no doubt. But of course there was more. The corporal punishment both at home and in school–automatic, unquestioned. Belts, paddles, sticks, for the least little thing. The executions in the news, all the grisly details, though often well deserved for heinous crimes, more grisly details. Three boys were butchered in a stable near our home. The killer wasn't charged until decades later. Kids in our area lived in fear for months, the forest around the stable strictly verboten. I, of course, had to go in, even spied on the stable hands. One of them turned out to be the killer. I had him pegged, saw him cracking a bullwhip. That decided it for me."

Astrid pulled back in her chair, amazed but amused.

"Did you tell anyone?"

"No. I wasn't supposed to be there. I didn't want to get punished myself."

"Well, I suppose your 'evidence' would not have been enough, anyway."

"Right. He'd already been questioned and had an alibi. It only fell apart by chance many years after."

"Was that it, then? The key influence toward your career, prior to the snake incident?"

"No, actually when very young I was attracted to the religious life, becoming a priest or monk or something. I guess I must have seen it as an escape at first. But then I realized there was evil there too, hiding behind the religious cloak. So instead I moved toward the social sciences, using what I learned to understand what I saw. I held many temporary jobs, observing the crude, aggressive, promiscuous behavior of less educated people. I noted the tendencies and saw them reflected in large-scale conflicts—tribal, sectarian, and political violence. The Vietnam war was then raging."

"Were you involved personally?"

"I was able to join the National Guard, a sort of on-call reserve for domestic unrest. I was in one deployment, patrolling inner-city streets after some riots."

"Chaos on top of war."

"Yes. Violence seemed to dominate the culture awhile, hanging around like a squatter afterward. I worked for the public aid department after graduating, saw its abysmal weakness as an institution. Families on the dole for generations, bunched in certain parts of the city and reinforcing each other's ignorance and hatreds, the cheapening of life and sexuality. After an interval I went for my master's degree, needing to study it all from a distance, keep my thinking in order, save my intelligence and my sanity."

"And yet here you are, looking to get closer than ever to things, sharing your desire with a policewoman."

"Well, a detective."

She smiled as she sometimes did in the bedroom. With the additional light, however, the luster of her golden hair, her expression was more strikingly sweet. I didn't want to think of her in the police, the danger, the increased risk of my losing her.

"What are you thinking?" she finally asked. "You look like you did before, when I was cooking."

I leaned forward against the table.

"I was thinking about what you said, getting closer than ever to things. With Rinai, with this suspect, the evidence at hand, I don't know if it's enough, actually. The central problem, the core evil, I always knew was quite remote. Now I wonder if it's unreachable. Despite all its many manifestations."

"Maybe you need to go there."

"Where?"

"New Guinea or wherever. Borneo, Sumatra. The place that got Sven in trouble."

"He was already in trouble. But, now that you mention it–"

I stopped and envisioned the distance, the contrast in climate, the vagueness of final destination. Vague, too, would be my purpose to the ears of those I'd meet, those I would depend on. On the other hand, I'd been to the area before, would not be going in cold, could leave whenever I wished or saw necessary, or if things just weren't working out.

"I don't know," I said to Astrid. "That might be quite a project. More to it than the hop over here to Scania."

"I'd like to go myself," she said, "but there's Nils to go through, and the chief, and they would say no at this point."

I was struck by the bizarreness of her idea.

"Are you that much interested in pursuing this thing to its source?" I asked her.

She looked at me with calm assurance.

"You're right about evil," she said. "It runs through history, imbues itself in customs and beliefs. I think it inspires people toward disorder and destruction, ugliness and depravity, disease. We're up against nihilists in the end, cult followers of a maniac from hell. We have no choice, people like you and me, but to fight them. And to fight *It*."

⚒⚒

I spent the day before the trial in Astrid's apartment, she at work as usual, but we'd agreed I should spend that night in my hotel room. Nils might call there to settle something for our drive, and it would be easier for me in the morning. I had a walk at lunchtime, taking the meal in a simple café, and was gratified that no one recognized me. It seemed I'd successfully avoided the news coverage of the killings and the suspect. On returning to the apartment, I checked my email and found a message from Midori requesting that I call. I promptly did so.

"There's been an incident or two," she informed me after our greetings.

"Serious?"

"The worst and close to worst."

"Go on."

"Rinai was out by herself one evening, an issue by itself I guess, but we heard later about something happening, something big. A man staying in a motel nearby, an out-of-towner attending a conference, was found dead in his room. Unknown cause, but there was evidence someone had been with him. Food and beverage remains, a female voice heard. The prelude and the death were during Rinai's sojourn from the Center."

"Bad," I commented, "very bad. Did the police make contact there?"

"Not yet. I don't think they've seen a connection. Rinai hasn't said anything and the workers don't want to believe, so they're close-mouthed too. I don't know about Gruner."

"He'd be in denial. It's a nascent catastrophe."

"Yes, well, he's a problem for us himself, I'm afraid. That's the other thing I have to tell you. He's taken to bad-mouthing you at meetings, blaming you for any problems the Center is facing. At the same time, he's bringing in another flock of cases, a half-dozen or more. Eating disorders, split personalities, dumb stuff like that. Mostly idle housewives, I expect. Bart sits there nodding and smiling, thinking cash flow heals all. I'd say we're facing a leadership crisis."

"How are you holding up yourself?"

"Personally? I'm okay, people don't bother me. Something in me warns them off, I guess. Except you. And I miss you, of course."

"Same here, my lovely. We'll make it up strongly when I get back. But, you know, there's a new twist come up on Rinai that might delay my return."

"Oh? What is it?"

I heard her professional self return, our relationship back on hold. I was gratified by this, proceeded to an account of my interviews and the linkage of Tapunui to the "cult of Kakili." I gave credit to Nils, held off mentioning Astrid.

"Were you thinking of talking to the suspect?" Midori asked.

"He's shielded by lawyers, was hardly talking anyway. The trial's tomorrow, some distance from here. We leave at the crack of dawn."

"So where's the delay you mentioned? You expect a long trial?"

"No, not that. What it is, I'm thinking of chasing down that Kakili connection. If we can locate a specific person or place with links to both Rinai and Tapunui, we should be at the source or portal of the evil orchestrating these crimes."

"Sounds like you're thinking of another long trip. And a dangerous one."

"It might be well worth it, though. We'd have something

to confront Rinai with, as well as material for the police to use in preventing more killings. It might even be a boon to the Center's reputation."

Midori was silent a moment.

"I guess you're rather set on it," she said.

I realized then that I was, albeit with details to work out, precautions to take. I'd be moving on, I had momentum, but it all might look different from Midori's perspective.

"Perhaps I'm getting carried away," I said. "I don't want to be selfish in this, leaving you there with Rinai for a longer time and all. We could always attend to her case without my traveling on it."

"Hey, no," Midori responded. "I don't want to be a wet blanket. Follow your nose. 'If you got a hunch, bet a bunch,' as the old gambler would say."

"Whoa!" I chuckled. "Aphorisms from both barrels."

"Really, now. Don't worry about me. Anyway, Rachel's the assigned worker so I have a buffer there. Gruner's own doing, right?"

"Sure. And how is Rachel doing with Rinai?"

"Getting totally played. She's young, believes anything. But don't worry, I'll guard against further disasters. You can trust me."

"Trust? Of course I trust you, Midori. I will always trust you."

━┅┅┅┅⫸┆⫷┅┅┅┅━

Sitting in the lobby of my hotel, awaiting the early pickup by Nils, I felt some regret at having spent the night there. I hadn't slept well away from Astrid, knowing that she was near but we were each of us alone. It felt quite unnatural. I told myself that it was necessary, the classic exercise of will. I told myself it didn't matter in the great, panoramic scheme of things. I sensed a sluggish response from the memory in my flesh and bones: the dull grunt of anger as from a heavy primitive beast, overriding the rational, the purposeful. But then there was Nils, revolving through the doors and striding over the just-vacuumed carpet, leaving fresh dents in it. Footprints but indistinct, like those for corroborating my testimony in the trial.

We exchanged greetings, joked about the early start, moved on to the car.

"About the footprints," I said as we drove, "just how exact a match were they? I mean, being in the mud and all."

"Well, we couldn't capture every scratch and ding on the soles. The softness of the mud had smoothed them over. It was also too soft for us to take impressions. All we have are photos and our measurements, but there's nothing there that disqualifies them from being the suspect's."

I mulled this over, found it weak.

"And the bolo, or machete. No good prints at all?"

"No. Smudged somewhat to begin with, then splattered with mud and rained on."

"But its location suggests it was discarded by the killer."

"Correct. In relation to the footprints and their direction."

It began to rain, lightly but steadily, the windshield wipers at half-speed. I thought of the other witnesses, two tramps and a railway worker Tapunui had clobbered. I thought about their credibility and the value of their testimony. They'd supposedly seen him stow away on a freight train, but so what? Would that even begin to be evidence without my positive identification? Of course not.

"When were the photos of the suspect taken?" I asked.

"Day of his arrest. Standard procedure."

"They were officially dated?"

"Of course."

Nils glanced over from behind the wheel.

"As we said before, though, he'll look different in court."

"Sure," I acknowledged.

The rain came down a little harder and we drove mostly in silence. We were uneasy but not about the weather. Even if the rain changed to snow, we'd be at our destination before it became a problem. Our discomfort arose from a new unpredictability about the trial, or rather one we hadn't realized before. Nils had seemed to have a clear vision of what could happen, the charges and evidence and judicial options. But now, on the decisive day, it seemed the case might look shaky to the official judge and be open to various attacks by the defense. We'd assumed support from the lay judges, but how competent could they be in such a rural district? The prosecutor might well find himself adrift, clinging to my distant identification as a lifebuoy. I could only hope that the lay judges, in deference to their community's safety, would strongly argue in our favor.

"We're coming to the town," Nils informed me.

The car jolted over a railroad crossing, dispelling the drowsiness that had recurred in me. We passed a scattering of shops and service stations and were soon in the main business district, in the middle of which was the old stone court building. All was quiet under the gloomy sky, the rain abating now to a drizzle, but there was a goodly number of cars near the building, along with a waiting ambulance, lights and siren off.

"In case he flips out," Nils quipped.

We entered the building and passed through a sprinkling of discreetly chatting people en route to the courtroom entrance. Near the heavy doors a smartly dressed woman called out to Nils, who stepped over to talk with her. He returned to me with a troubled look on his face.

"She's assistant prosecutor," he said. "Her boss cut a deal on Sven's case. Dropped the charge in exchange for a deportation agreement."

"So it's down to John's case only."

"Right. But there's more."

He looked away and grimaced, ground his teeth for a second.

"One of the lay judges was murdered last night."

"What!"

"He was inspecting his stables, took a blow to the head. They threw him in one of the stalls to make it seem like a horse kicked him. Trouble was, the horse of choice was an old gelding, kept around out of sentiment. Plus the wound didn't match a horse's hoof."

I was silent a moment, absorbing and processing.

"So, can the trial still go on today?"

"Probably, as long as the other two lay judges are in agreement. They're back in chambers now thrashing it out."

"Will the case for the prosecution be affected?"

"It shouldn't be. But the thing last night had a purpose, an evil purpose. It wasn't any coincidence coming just before the trial."

"A warning? A threat?"

"I've seen it before," Nils said resignedly.

It was announced that the judges were coming out. People crowded through the doors and assumed their seats in the courtroom, the center chair for the lay judges conspicuously vacant. I saw a man at the defense table who apparently was the defendant, but now with a haircut and clean-shaven, as well as decently dressed. I wasn't sure how or even if I could justify my identification. As it turned out, however, I wasn't asked to. The official judge, after announcing the plea deal in Sven's case, announced another in John's case. For pleading guilty to my friend's murder, Tapunui was sentenced to seven years' imprisonment, but with the sentence suspended to allow for immediate deportation.

Nils and myself, along with others from the courthouse, processed this outcome at the nearest tavern with the rain intensifying beyond the windows.

VI.

While she was unable to accompany me, and I wouldn't have wished her to, Astrid was with me in spirit as I traveled to the archipelagoes. Gentle as it was, her encouragement was needed for me to do what was now clearly necessary. With the help of a regional professor with whom I'd once collaborated, I'd locate the nexus of the violence I'd seen and identify the chief perpetrator. Whether led by Kakili or common criminal, the evil network had to be destroyed, its insidious influence ended.

Arriving in Kuala Lumpur, I splurged on an upscale hotel to rest from the long flight and for the impending quest. I used the Center's credit card as I had with the airline. My research colleague, Vic Barangan, would arrive from Port Moresby the following day. In the hotel dining room, with the attention of an attractive hostess, it seemed I was still a world apart from the dread reality I sought. The scattering of other guests, mostly other travelers, chattered blissfully, oblivious to the deep concerns that shaded my own outlook. Later, as I looked out over the city from my suite, the lights and patterns below appeared a grand web of illusions. Even here, though geographically close, humanity ignored the corrupting force extending its reach to them from its subterranean haunts.

I was reading in the lobby next day when Professor

Barangan arrived as expected. He'd put on weight and aged noticeably since last I'd seen him. We exchanged greetings, commented on the heat outside, and proceeded to the bar for cocktails. He had no need to register since there was a sofa bed in my suite.

"So," Vic said when we were settled, "we collaborate again."

"Yes," I responded, "but not for publication. At least not on my end. That's my employer's call."

"And you said she's a patient, the young woman. So, discretion."

"As much as possible, yes. Though there's that overriding priority: the need to disrupt a network of violence , neutralize its source if possible."

Vic's eyebrows rose.

"'Make no small plans,' as someone said."

"We can't afford to. There's too much at stake."

"And the police, in your view, really can't handle it?"

"They haven't so far. I've seen it up close. The evil is wanton, mocking the law and the attempts to enforce it."

"Yes, so much of that. Across cultures and generations, across the earth. Violence towards people and property, anarchy, internecine conflicts, senseless wars. People ask where will it end, but the question should be where does it begin. Correct?"

"Well, they have the stock answers. Human nature, social injustice, poverty, ignorance, fanaticism. But even with those addressed, the chaos goes on, increases."

"Because those aren't really causes, they're symptoms. Outcroppings of much larger evils that are hidden, potential killers. The person who commits misdemeanors in response to conditions and is excused will advance to felonies and become a social condition himself. Evil preys on conditions that invite it, recruits its self-righteous agents and grows in strength through them."

"And, of course, since civilization is never perfect, there are always fissures of weakness to be preyed upon."

"Exactly."

"And so we seek the Source, one such source at least, perhaps a portal to regions unknown to humankind."

"Most of it, anyway."

I caught his suggestive glance. Was he thinking of us or the agents of Kakili as the exceptions? Either way or both, I saw that Vic and I shared a perspective on the existence and activity of those storied demons. I raised my glass.

"To our success, then."

"Complete and resounding," he agreed. "For now and the ages."

⊷⊰⊱✶⊰⊱⊷

We were mostly quiet on the short flight to Rinai's country, Vic studying my notes and other materials on her case. Our optimism in Kuala Lumpur might have been premature, I realized, since our plans were increasingly vague the further we progressed along our route. This was entirely my fault. In the effort to buoy and sustain my interest and confidence, I had focused mostly on the end result, imagined as a grand facing-down of the Kakili, an enhanced version of my youthful encounter with the cobra. But that had been a spontaneous experience in the midst of an otherwise banal field study, whereas the current goal required specific, deliberate steps leading up to the hoped-for conclusion.

"Time to get real," I thought out loud.

"How's that?" Vic looked up.

"I was thinking of the people we'll have to go through: the officials in the country itself, small and unpredictable, then those in the autonomous region, culturally distinct, then again

96

with her tribe, the extended clan. John said they were secretive and cultish, given to odd, outrageous practices."

Vic laughed.

"Right up our alley, isn't it? Professionally if not personally. Especially in this part of the world."

"I don't know. Seems we could run into obstacles."

"Well, your friend got through, didn't he? Sven?"

"John's friend, yes. But he had a professional agency paving the way."

"Professional? Hey, I know these parts better than any match-making service. If there are magic words to be spoken or palms to be greased, don't worry about it. I'll get us through fine."

As it turned out, we had a rather easy time at the airport. A female officer fished us out of the security line, leading us past the waiting locals for expedited service at the checkpoint, where our passports were stamped with little ado. We'd apparently been mistaken for commercial travelers, whom the small country wished to encourage. We rode in a tiny taxi through sun-baked streets, quiet for a capital, to a colonial-era hotel. It had a huge sitting room beyond the lobby with an open rear wall overlooking a brilliant, sizzling bay. Huge potted plants abounded, some actually trees, while here and there a small lizard scampered. This was the Sea Breeze Hotel.

"Not so many sea breezes today," Vic quipped.

The young man at the registration desk smiled, showing us his set of perfect-looking teeth. A credential for the job, I assumed. We stopped before ascending to our rooms for Vic to view the spacious salon, which I now noticed had tables for breakfast.

"We had a place like this in the Visayas," he commented.

"You miss being there?"

"Sometimes. Often, I suppose. But what can you do? You want a career, you must travel. The curse of the educated man."

We continued on to our rooms. After we'd rested and

washed up, we rejoined for a walk around the capital. The sun had declined somewhat but it was still quite warm. The tall palms afforded meager shade. We considered hiking to the palace, discussed the long return trip, decided instead to seek refreshment. The nondescript streets offered little in this department so we settled for fruity iced teas at a seedy outdoor café.

"He's quite young, the king here," Vic informed me. "Took over when his father was murdered."

"Oh? Who did it?"

"We don't really know. They executed someone, but he was just a tool at most. Gave no information."

"And the motive?"

"Also unknown."

I looked away under the faded table umbrella, felt the useless warm breeze, noted the lightness of street traffic. A deep uneasiness seemed to fester in this place.

"Is he in control of things, this boy-king?"

"As long as he pays the army well, though that cuts into other things. Education is a shambles, health care depends on foreign charities, and the roads, well–"

He gestured over the country as a whole.

"What about the autonomous zone?"

"They're mostly left to their own devices. Probably very corrupt if you looked into it, so best to not look into it. No doubt the threat of violence for any interference."

"And yet they leave Rinai's tribe alone, the extended clan."

"They're not so much tolerated as ostracized. They're like the old untouchables, physically and socially isolated, excluded over time for continuing with beliefs and practices that the larger society outgrew, rejected and found disgraceful."

"Among them allegiance to the cult of Kakili, perhaps even serving as its nexus."

"That well might be. Their ways are among the most primitive on earth, including along religious lines."

98

"Have you met anyone from the cult? Any contact at all?"

"Nothing to speak of. I've had someone pointed out to me once or twice. They're uncommunicative, as you know."

"Yes, like Tapunui. Though he's from back your way, apparently, rather than here. Which suggests, since he's involved in Rinai's situation, that–although dispersed–they can step out from their ancient ways and communicate long distance when they want to."

"Hm, yes. And, since they're dispersed, how can we know how many are out there? And *where* they are?"

"True, though it wouldn't take many to do a great deal of harm. We seem to have one in America who is proof of that."

"So we're back to finding the Source, to stopping things there."

"Yes, and by doing so closing a portal to even greater evils."

⊕⊷₿⊷⊀⊱₿⊷⊚

The following morning, we hired a driver for the day through the hotel. We'd specified knowledge of the autonomous zone and the driver, Ahmed, assured us that he knew it well, in fact had once lived there. We set off in a vintage American car with sporadic air conditioning, kept from being a classic by too many dents and do-it-yourself servicing. Ahmed was nonetheless proud of it, giving a blare of the horn to smaller vehicles, pedestrians, the occasional dog or goat. We were quickly out of the capital and passing rudimentary farms and wasteland.

There was little traffic on the road although we twice saw military vehicles, one coming from the direction we were headed and the other parked by a refreshment hut. The soldiers standing around appeared to be drinking beer. Ahmed slowed down to greet the proprietor, who shouted back and gestured for our driver to park. Ahmed shouted back and gestured toward us in the rear seat, then laughed and drove off, accelerating rapidly.

"We're VIP's," Vic quipped. "It's a small country."

There weren't many people in the fields, which were starting to bake, and most of those we saw were idling under the few ragged trees. Eventually the vegetation increased and then quickly became a jungle. Not long after, at a point where the trees thinned a bit, the main road swerved to the left while a lesser extension continued straight, with a gated official checkpoint a short distance ahead. A sign preceding the gate announced in several languages that we were now entering the autonomous zone and should have all papers ready.

"You have ten dollars American?" Ahmed asked.

"It's the strongest ticket," Vic explained.

I passed the note up to Ahmed. One of the guards, who seemed to know Ahmed and his car, came up to receive the gratuity. It was a friendly exchange.

"They are professors," Ahmed said. "They are studying our education."

"Professors?" the guard repeated slowly.

"Teachers!" Ahmed simplified.

The guard nodded and signaled a comrade to raise the gate. Our driver eased through and we were one stage closer to our quarry. The trees closed in again, their shade rather ineffectual, and we passed a couple of hamlets embedded in the jungle growth. After a long stretch we came to a larger settlement that looked like a slum that had been transplanted from some city. Ahmed turned into an alley that led to the far side of the village and out again into especially dark forest, becoming only a bumpy trail that declined into fetid humidity. Several young boys came into view, playing on the trail up ahead. Ahmed pulled off and parked on a relatively clear patch of ground.

"It's on foot from here," he said.

He got out of the car and we followed suit. The boys stopped in their play. Ahmed brought out a shiny coin and held it high. The boys came running up to him, the largest among them pushing the others away. Ahmed talked with this boy, holding the coin before his face and gesturing at Vic and myself.

"They're speaking the local dialect," Vic explained. "No English lessons recently."

Ahmed came over and handed me the coin.

"Give it to him when he takes you to the headman."

"Aren't you coming?"

"I prefer to wait here. If you are not back in thirty minutes I will come check on you."

His tone was purposeful. I was taken aback, the idea of coming this far for a half-hour interview seeming absurd. But I had to work with what was available and make what I could of it. In any event, I had little choice at this time.

"Only tip local money," Ahmed continued. "Don't waste your dollars on them."

"Sure," I agreed. "Let's go, Vic."

We went with the boys down a path that branched off the larger trail. It led to a group of weathered huts with one larger, less slummy house a bit removed. On its veranda sat a middle-aged man and woman in rattan chairs, both of them heavily built. The man sat up as we approached, curious, the woman continuing to fan herself. He wore faded cutoff shorts and was barefoot, nothing above the waist except a necklace of babirusa tusks. She wore a cheap floral wraparound, its effect on her appearance that of a sofa cover.

"Thank you," I said to the boy, and gave him Ahmed's coin.

Vic exchanged greetings with the couple, introducing me as an American philanthropist visiting the archipelagoes to learn people's needs.

"We need everything," the woman asserted. "We have two governments and they both give us nothing."

The headman nodded, his expression otherwise vacant.

"I'm very sorry to hear that," I politely responded.

A few other people had gathered nearby, but they stayed well clear of the veranda. Another man, however, came around the side of the house and stood right next to me. He appeared to be about thirty, with newer shorts than the headman plus sandals, and he had abstract tattoos covering his face and shoulders.

"This is our priest," the headman stated. "He can discuss with you." He then said something to the priest in their dialect.

"Come," the younger man said, and walked back in the direction he'd come from.

Vic and I followed. The priest's hut was a little farther from the main group than the headman's. It had been painted black at one time but had faded to gray and was chipping. A pair of skulls impaled on poles stood on either side of the entrance. They'd somehow been stained indigo but this too was fading. The priest gestured for us to sit on a bench under an awning on one side of the house. As I did so, I noticed what appeared to be washed-out bandages hanging from a line strung between trees.

"I am also the doctor here," the priest explained. "My name is Zel."

Vic and I introduced ourselves.

"Did you bring offering?" the priest-doctor asked.

I was still processing the question when Vic brought out some domestic banknotes. Being an academic, he was familiar with honorariums.

"So," Zel continued, "headman says you study needs."

I was acutely conscious of time being short and a need to be direct if I were to learn anything here.

"The fact is," I asserted, "I'm now servicing the needs of one of your people, a young woman who left here six or seven moths ago. Her name is Rinai. She's now in America by way of Sweden. Her husband died and she is in a special clinic to help her adjustment. She has stated some memories and beliefs that we do not understand, so any information you can give would help us to help *her*."

He listened calmly, showing only mild interest.

"What are these 'memories and beliefs?'"

I summarized the narratives pf Sven, John, and Rinai herself, minimizing the violent incidents but needing to touch on them to elicit Zel's interest, get the fullest possible response from him. He listened without interrupting, the occasional small frown his only reaction. When I finished he smiled sardonically.

"Yes, she was here, this Rinai. One of the restless young girls, eager to get away, perhaps the most eager. A nuisance. The headman approved to get rid of her. The zone guards came about her husband's death, but we knew nothing. The Kakili is a figure of legend, a myth, though some cling to belief as some do with all myths. Look at this place here, hardly a village. Do you think we would live like this if we had a great power?"

I gazed toward the battered huts, could not answer him.

"But what about the deaths?" Vic asked. "The killings?"

"The ones not showing violence might be natural. People are always dying. The ones that were violent, yes, there was evil intent, perhaps evil agency. But you had this Sven, correct? He was the one who sought out Rinai, sought some connection here, perhaps Kakili. You should study this husband, his own interest in the powers."

I thought of my visit to Frans and Tuva, its apparent unimportance at the time. Had bloodlust been gestating in Sven's family for generations? And now, with the continued violence, had the aura of malevolence passed from Sven to Rinai upon his death?

"We appreciate your talking with us," I said to Zel. "Is there anything more you can tell us about Rinai or her intentions?"

He appeared to reflect a moment.

"There is the ziggurat, a temple down the road, two kilometers or so. It is a connection to the Kakili, some believe."

"Thank you. We'll look at it."

We took our leave of the priest-doctor, saluting the headman and consort as we passed their veranda. I looked around as we walked among the sorry huts, trying to imagine Rinai living here, day after day, month after month. I couldn't. Even with the addition of a distinctive cultural feature, actual belief in the Kakili or something similar, the place would retain a crushing banality that couldn't possibly nurture the devious, darkly charming, dangerous persona of Rinai. She'd been restless, the priest-doctor had said, but it seemed her true self had bloomed only after her departure, in response to later influence, in response to Sven.

"One more stop, then?" Vic asked.

"Yes, the ziggurat. We'll have Ahmed get as close as he can."

We found him lounging on the car's back seat, smoking, all the car's doors open for air.

"Wouldn't it be more comfortable under a tree?" I asked him.

"Not once the ants found you. They are killers here. Also the snakes."

He seemed a bit woozy, gave me a blank look as I explained our next step, but he put the car in gear and bounced off along the ersatz road. We soon sighted the ziggurat in a small clearing down an overgrown approach path. Ahmed surprisingly sprang out of the car and went around to the foot of the path. He was kicking and poking at the obstructing weeds as Vic and I approached and joined him.

"I will go first," he said. "Just stop where you see I am stopping."

We followed his directions and were soon within a few feet of the ziggurat, a rectangular stone tower with walls sloping inward toward a flat roof with irregular surface, as if some crowning structure had been destroyed. It was perhaps forty feet high. Some wire webbing, like that used for flimsy fences, was fastened across the entrance, but the window openings were only about five feet off the ground. We therefore had a good view of the interior. Tree litter and some animal bones could be seen, along with bird and bat droppings, but what dominated the scene was a wide pit in the center of the dirt floor. From the straightness of its sides it appeared to be quite deep, while an eerie light emanated from below.

"Phosphorescence?" I queried Vic.

"I sure hope so," he laughed.

"They used this for ceremonies," said Ahmed. "The ones back there." A nod towards Rinai's people. "Maybe still do."

"What's that stink?" Vic asked.

"Animals get in and fall in the hole. Also the bats drop dead off the ceiling. Don't go in or they get excited and unload on you. Also they are vampires."

Vic abruptly backed away.

"Are we done here, I hope?"

But Ahmed wasn't finished.

"There are stories about something living down there, a giant rat or many of them. In a tunnel going all the way to Sumatra, or straight down into the earth. That would be worse, of course."

"Something not natural," I thought aloud.

"Yes, sir."

We lingered a short time longer, examining the structure's exterior, sharing a growing repulsion. I could easily imagine the cult of Kakili here, the ceremonies being their sacrifices. The tribe and their activities were beyond the purview of civil authorities. Communication between cultists over long distances, whether through a fantastic tunnel or more modern means, would eventually cause problems for the outside world. With a willing potential agent in a developed Western country, someone like Sven, the cult's advancement could be greatly accelerated.

The day's heat had grown intense, the insect song shrill, and a bird of prey circled above, then two. We drifted away from the ziggurat, back towards the car, then got in.

Vic was engaged for the evening with an academic contact, so I dined alone at a restaurant near the hotel. Most of the other patrons were well-off locals. The meal was rather dull, as was the walk from the hotel and back, so I was left with the sticky web of my own thoughts. I wasn't convinced that I'd learned all I might about Rinai's origins. At the same time, this wasn't an inviting place to look for answers. It was a land of dead ends, seductive wrong turns, confusing factions struggling for minor empowerment. The atmosphere here was like the cloud surrounding Sven and Rinai from the beginning, full of vagaries but with no genuine enlightenment. I had to get out, I thought, retrace my steps, apply myself assiduously to detail, gain the truer view that comes with a second look.

Alone in my room later, restless, I was able to reach Midori by phone. Something in my voice must have alerted her because she asked if I was all right.

"Healthwise, yes," I answered. "With the situation, well, I don't know."

"You're still looking for Rinai's contacts? And the portal of evil, I think you said?"

"I might've been a bit carried away by my expectations. I found where she'd lived, all right, but it could've been hundreds of other places. As for the 'portal of evil,' try a hole in the floor of an old temple. Not much better than finding a derelict outhouse."

"Well, at least you checked things out. You found what *didn't* make her like she is."

"Maybe. Thing is, there were still suggestions, nuances, in what we saw, leaving the possibility that there is after all some connection, or that there *was* but the evil moved on with Rinai, leaving only a charged atmosphere."

"Hm, interesting. So you'll be hanging on with this awhile?"

"Yes, I think so. Anyway, we have her case there to service, right?"

"True Your gaining background on her is entirely justified. To me, anyway. But listen, I have to tell you something. Did you bring your personal credit card with you? Not just the Center's?"

"Sure. I always have it with me. Why?"

"Well, Gruner's been having more meetings, trying to get a handle. It's been like a circus with all the new cases. He skips around different subjects, looking or hoping for answers, including on the financial side. Bart's baby, of course, his chance to shine. Anyway, while holding the floor, Bart brings up the expenses on Rinai's case. Specifically, your travel and miscellaneous charges to the Center's credit account. They sounded high there in the meeting and this last one came off as questionable. Gruner was really nettled. He told Bart to suspend or cancel the account, make it useless for charging."

"So, I'm on my own now on this, financially speaking."

"Afraid so. I tried an objection, but it had no effect."

"Well, thanks for trying, Midori."

"And there's something else." She hesitated. "Actually more important, what I needed much more to let you know."

"Just so I still have your love. Lay it on me."

"It's not about *my* feelings for you, it's about *theirs*. As that meeting ended, Gruner floated the idea of a vote among the charter members, Rudy now having John's vote. Measure to be voted on: your exclusion from the group!"

Despite Midori's news, I slept rather well. The trip into the A-Zone, with its accompanying heat, had induced a growing fatigue that forestalled anxiety. Awakening with the daylight, I felt refreshed except for a stiffness that testified to the depth of my sleep. My predilection for strong coffee set in so I decided to consult Vic about breakfast. On dialing his room number, however, I heard only a series of rings and a recorded message that the guest was not answering. It occurred to me that Vic had not come in by the time I'd gone to bed, so I hadn't seen him since Ahmed had dropped me at the hotel and driven off with Vic to his academic contact. I knocked on the door of his room on my way to breakfast, but to no avail.

I ate in the huge room off the lobby with its open rear wall overlooking the bay. The day's heat had not yet settled in earnest so there was in fact a soft sea breeze, assisted by ceiling fans high overhead and so justifying the hotel's name. The ubiquitous tiny lizards kept me company, scampering with buzz-like chirps between the huge potted plants. Except for ants in the marmalade the breakfast was entirely adequate. I moved upon finishing to an armchair by the airy non-wall.

I had no idea how to process Midori's news. If things were as bad at the Center as she described, there wasn't much I could do there. As for the threatened vote, considering the charter members and their loyalties and fears, it seemed I had only Midori on my side for the tally. On the other hand, with the investigation of Rinai, I sensed there was a way forward. "Study this husband," Zel the priest-doctor had said, study Sven's pre-Rinai "interest in the powers." I still had Frans and Tuva as resources, despite the poor output from our one interview. And perhaps there were records of some sort, or something unforeseen would present itself. Such were my thoughts as I reclined before the warming bay, my head back and ceiling fans pulsating above me. I was soon asleep.

I became aware of a hand shaking me by the shoulder. My first thought was of Vic finally risen from his slumber. The face that came into view, however, was new to me and somber, topped by a cap with braided trim. Another face was slightly distant, also with cap but no braid. Two men dressed in khaki, awaiting my consciousness.

"I am Captain Edward," said the first officer. "The hotel informs us you arrived with Victor Barangan."

"Yes, I did. I'm waiting just now for him to come down."

The captain glanced at the other officer.

"He will not be coming down, sir. He was killed last night in a traffic accident."

"What!"

"On the coastal road. His driver missed a turn. They went through the guard rail and down into the bay."

I was near-speechless, only the most obvious question occurring to me.

"Was the driver maned Ahmed?"

"No, sir. He was a professor from our university. His family identified both bodies. There had been a dinner earlier, alcohol consumed."

"And the time," I thought to ask, "what time was it?"

"Between midnight and one o'clock."

I said nothing, picturing myself asleep then.

"What we need to do," said Capt. Edward, "is to contact your associate's family. Do you have an address or phone number for them?"

"No. Those would be with his employer in Port Moresby, the College of St. Anselm."

"His family is in that country?"

"No. They are in the Visayas, where he came from. I don't know exactly where."

The captain questioned his companion, who was scribbling on a pad. The other officer nodded a brief answer.

"Well, sir," the captain said to me, "I think we are done here. Would you have a business card, by chance?"

I fished one out of my wallet. He raised an eyebrow as he read it, slowly nodding.

"Extreme Dysfunction," he read aloud. "We could use such a place here." Then, pocketing the card: "Our condolences on your loss, doctor. We will work with the family regarding the body and the belongings. Good day."

The two men left my field of vision, their footsteps receding toward the front of the building. I was left with the blazing bay and the great nothingness above. I'd fly into it next day, again alone, chagrined at my involvement of Vic in the less than fruitful quest. Yet I still felt a sense of purpose, because there had to be purpose to balance the oppressive chaos of the universe, some resistance to the steady influx of evil.

VII.

Astrid again met me at the airport in Malmo, this time at a more reasonable hour, the early evening. It was nonetheless dark, owing to the time of year, and shockingly cold to me coming straight from the tropics. We stopped at a quieter sort of pub where I related my misadventures and she told of the aftermath of the Tapunui verdict. Right-wing militants had stepped up their recruiting, the press delighting with new stories to cover, and discouragement was heavy at her department and others.

"Nils is more cynical than ever," she said.

"Oh? At the trial he seemed to expect what happened."

"Not just basically walking free. Not for a crime like *that*."

"No, I suppose not."

"Another nail in the coffin of optimism. My father warned me about it."

"Not that far off reality, it seems."

Astrid gave me a sympathetic look. In the candlelight she looked too wonderful to be real, absurdly angelic after the stinking pit of the Kakili.

"Sorry about your friend down there," she said. "I feel like comforting you. Here. Now."

"That might be a little awkward. How about we go with delayed gratification?"

"Sure. It's *your* homecoming."

111

I recalled her saying something like that before, when I'd returned to testify at the trial. I watched her sip her drink, look out over others in the pub, enjoy the ambience, enjoy being with me. The question returned as to whether it was time to relax, not just a little but a lot, relegate the old obsession-compulsion to a back seat on the trip. Emeritus status. Wasn't there a point where, no matter how much or how little you'd accomplished, you'd acquitted yourself well and that was that? But that would be in the judgment of others, I realized, totally separate from my own satisfaction, approval, acceptance as truth. Until that point was reached, I needed to persevere against the still extant adversary.

"Like another drink?" I inquired.

"Well, there's wine at the apartment."

We'd never had more than one cocktail together, following instead with wine and usually a meal. Another mutual habit setting in, I reflected, circumscribing our potential future.

"Sounds good," I said. "Any time you're ready."

It turned out that Astrid had a poached salmon dinner to heat up in the oven. She'd foreseen that I'd be hungry due to the airlines' new frugality, but not in the mood for a restaurant. My sense of circumscription was further accentuated, but I decided to let it go. I was amused, charmed, felt secure with this young woman. She still appeared delicate, especially in this domestic setting, yet there was the knowledge that she was a police detective, as aware as I was, I thought, of the viciousness in the world.

"It's been a while since I asked about your work," I said. "Too wrapped up in my own, maybe. How's it been going?"

"Oh, the same kind of mix, basically, only more of it. Domestic abuse, store thefts, missing persons, school incidents. I've noticed a sort of change, though, among our people, a malaise. There's a subtle, hostile twist to the infractions, actual sadism in more serious ones. Maybe I'm imagining it, but people seem less healthy, less stable, not as capable of clear thinking, judgments, remembering positive values. As if something is creeping through our society, infecting it. And beyond, out over the planet."

"You see this consistently, all the time?"

"Yes, perhaps increasingly."

"And it wasn't just there all the time and you didn't notice it?"

"No, I don't think it's disillusionment."

"Of course it isn't."

"Of course?"

"Yes. There's clearly been a breakdown recently, a breach in the barriers against negative forces in human and other natures. The weakness in leadership, less intelligent and low character people holding high office, allows a confluence of evil forces to run rampant through city and countryside. Rioting is promoted as social protest, buildings burnt down or blanketed with obscene graffiti, the wrongdoers going unpunished. Criminals are coddled as celebrities, police attacked as if *they* are the criminal element. Contagious diseases go unabated, partisan politicians refusing to respect science. Sectarian and racial bigotry is embraced as virtue, some claiming to be victims while practicing it themselves, with threats and extortion or actual violence. Then there are the charlatans, the corruption, the wars–"

"Yes, the wars. The endless wars, so senseless."

"Anarchy. And yet, within the splashes of anarchy, widespread, there's unified purpose."

"An evil purpose."

"Right. The purpose being evil itself, its regeneration and growth. It creates anarchy and feeds on it, grows stronger from the negative nourishment, ever more degenerate, able to create greater anarchy, on which it feeds again in its expanding cycle of degenerate regeneration."

Astrid held up a hand.

"Wait! That rings a bell. Didn't Rinai say to you or John that the Kakili 'consumes the darkness?'"

I thought a moment.

"Yes, and we thought it could be metaphorical, the darkness being negative human qualities. Maybe also the people controlled by them."

"Well, then. There you are! The Kakili consuming darkness is what you just described, the nourishment of evil to create more of itself, increase and spread its power. The cycle is complete and continuing, the snake swallowing its tail though the tail grows ever longer."

I sat back in my chair.

"I believe that symbol is taken. But yes, I see your point. And we seem to be in the middle of things. With the deaths, with Rinai, with so much that's unknown."

"But we know there's a pattern."

"Yes, a pattern. So, next step, fill in the details."

"And your starting point, Mr. Investigator?"

"Well, there's a certain apartment full of antiques. We've both been there, at different times. But I've a feeling there was much more to be learned there than either of us got. I'd say Frans and Tuva, along with her collection, are worth a long second look."

⊷⊷⊱⊰⊶⊷

Astrid had requested leave for the day after my return, so she was free to accompany me on my visit to Frans and Tuva. We'd decided that their seeing both of us would add to our element of surprise, increase our chances of eliciting something useful. Astrid drove to their upscale neighborhood and parked a block from their building. We could thus approach inconspicuously on foot. When seen from some distance, the building appeared to have been converted from a commercial structure, thus accounting for the unusual spaciousness of the apartments. They were no doubt in demand in this artistic and academic community.

We were admitted by Frans, who was predictably flabbergasted.

"We missed you at the trial," said Astrid, as if she'd been there herself. "We thought we'd fill you in on the situation."

"I'm afraid Tuva stepped out."

"Oh, sorry we missed her. Maybe you can pass the information along."

"Sure."

"May we sit down?"

"Of course."

We'd no sooner sat down than I requested to use the restroom. Frans directed me to it, fortunately located at the furthest reach of the apartment. This allowed me to do a surreptitious inspection of Tuva's collection while Astrid occupied Frans with minutiae. I had her tiny camera in my pocket in case something stood out, but I was also wary of Tuva springing out from some hiding place to thwart my efforts.

I slowed my pace as I waded into the all-covering display of artifacts, exhibiting at first only a normal show of curiosity. I passed the cutting weapons, looking for similarity to Tapunui's bolo, but his had been plain and most of these were ornate. The masks and headdresses were also on the fancy side, along with some shields I hadn't noticed before. One of the shields, I noted, bore an abstract pattern virtually identical to Zel the priest-doctor's tattooing. I furtively snapped a picture of it, along with a wall hanging that had obscene images redolent of the Kakili cult. I passed over the jewelry items strung with small bones, not sighting any babirusa, but was attracted by a princess's wedding necklace of small silver coins, Dutch and eighteenth century. Rinai had worn earrings that were a perfect complement. Continuing back past stuffed birds of paradise, I saw miniature iron stoves that could be used for burning incense or, supposedly, mixtures of herbs. I was reminded of Rinai's sacrifices but saw no further significance.

It occurred to me that I should give some indication of using the restroom, so I rounded the bend by a huge ceremonial drum to give the toilet a flush. I stopped short, however, on seeing a large box of bones by the restroom door. Among the contents were three skulls, to my eye human, two tinted amber and the third a glowing red. Their colors were fresher than the blue pair owned by Zel, but then his were exposed to the elements. I assumed there'd been another red one, apparently a successful sale for Tuva on the Internet.

The flush accomplished, I took stock of the remaining rooms. I'd passed the kitchen and seen nothing unusual except a large amount of redundant cookware–woks, kettles, cauldrons, and such. That left the two bedrooms, one with its door forbiddingly shut. I judged it highly probable that the reclusive Tuva was coiled within, that my entry would risk an enraged strike, so I turned instead to the room with its door ajar. I found that it clearly was used for storage, filled with the nondescript junk that storerooms usually hold, but with one curious idiosyncrasy. A shelving unit in the far corner was draped with a heavy black cloth, as if to decisively set it off from the mundane jumble it stood beyond. I naturally picked my way over to it and lifted the cloth. I saw a phalanx of large jars almost filling the unit's shelves, their contents at first not clear since suspended in cloudy liquid. On better discerning the details, however, I realized that each jar contained a foetal or baby pig, the coloring and budding tusks suggesting that these were babirusas. I let fall the cloth and gingerly backed away.

Once out of the room, processing what I'd seen, I thought

that whatever the other bedroom held would be anticlimactic. It was diminished in my view and so I no longer feared having a peek. With extreme caution, I turned the knob and opened the door a small fraction of an inch. I looked in. Tuva was not there, only a simple and cheap-looking bedroom arrangement: carelessly made double bed, two upright chairs, bureau with toilet items atop. The walls were bare. The latter detail struck me as odd, given the conditions in the other rooms, but overall I found the room devoid of interest. I closed the door and proceeded to rejoin Astrid and Frans.

"Everything all right?" he asked humanely.

"Yes. No real problem."

"Good. This weather lately, things going around."

I nodded assent. Given the time I'd been gone, I assumed there was little I could add to the information provided by Astrid, our purported reason for visiting. I looked to her for a cue on this, but she only gave her professional smile.

"Are we done here, then?" I ventured.

She nodded tightly and we rose to depart.

"So what do you think of him?" she asked as we left the building.

"I think he's someone who made a mistake in life and is still suffering the results."

"Something like Sven?"

"No. Sven knew what he was doing, and his fate was much quicker."

We passed a few arty and student types as we walked to the car.

"Like to stop for some crêpes?" Astrid asked. "There's a nice place for them by that next intersection."

"All right."

We continued walking in a rare splash of sunlight. She asked if I'd learned anything in my tour of Tuva's collection, if I'd taken any pictures, so I gave her an accounting. I hesitated in describing the contents of the jars behind the black cloth, considering we were about to have lunch, but then went ahead. We were professionals, after all.

"You didn't take a picture of that, did you?"

"No. I guess I probably should have."

"Never mind. Your description is plenty."

The lunch was quite pleasant, welcome diversion after my disturbing trip and the low point of Tuva's collection. It was difficult to set aside the work, though, and on some level neither of us wanted to. Astrid informed me that deportation proceedings on Tapunui had stalled, the identity of his home country in dispute, no place receptive to taking him except the U.S., barred because of capital punishment.

"So he's still held by Immigration?"

"Yes, but not in their facility here. He's in the big prison up in Kumla. Maximum security."

"Any chance it might not go through? The deportation?"

"Well, they've had the problem before but it's always been worked out, as far as I know. As a last resort, there's some tiny countries that might take him for cash. Lots of it, of course."

An idea came to me.

"You know, there are some states in the U.S. that have banned capital punishment. The Center I work for is in one of them. If I proposed to bring him in as a medical case, like with Rinai, maybe Immigration would release him to me."

Astrid was taken aback.

"Why in the world would you want to do *that*?"

"To get at his knowledge of the Kakili and the network of evil embracing the world."

"Like you have with Rinai?" A small sardonic smile.

"He could add to what we've gotten from her. He might be quite forthcoming if properly worked on."

"What would your medical basis be? He was judged sane for the trial here."

"Yes, that's a problem. Perhaps a new evaluation, one by our Dr. Gruner."

"There'd be a thing about bias, conflict of interest. And what about your *federal* authorities? Couldn't they just swoop in and haul him off to execution territory?"

"That gets complicated. But okay, I see your point. Points. I was just thinking we might float the idea somewhere, see what happens. It's a reach, I know."

Astrid looked pained.

"It's a little more than a reach, I think. I can't see the people involved–*any* of them, frankly–going along with it. Except Tapunui himself, I suppose."

An awakened expression suddenly lit her face. I sensed she had hit on something, then tapped into her thoughts, a fog lifting from my own.

"Tapunui cooperating," I said, "carrot-on-stick."

She nodded, face still bright.

"Using my crazy plan as the carrot," I added.

"Yes, and getting as much from him here as you would by dragging him to America."

⊛⊷⥱⊷⊰⊷⥵⊷⊶⊕

There was a Friday evening commuter flight to Kumla, which enabled Astrid to accompany me to the big prison. She was almost a necessity, an ersatz interpreter for Tapunui's pidgin Swedish, his only communication except his obscure Melanesian dialect. We'd reserved a room in a modest hotel in the town, checked the Saturday visitation hours, and told no one about our plan. Astrid would use her police credentials to skirt any maximum security issues.

We had a smooth short flight and a relaxing evening, but were awakened in the night by the sound of many motorcycles roaring along the street below. Astrid was up first, her silhouette by the window clear to me as I rose to consciousness. I got up to join her, my arm over her shoulders as we watched the road mob barrel along, feeling free to drive over sidewalks and disregard traffic signals, knock over any object that wasn't secured.

"Which are they?" I asked. "Right wing or left?"

"Could be either," she said, "or neither one. There's also anarchists, racialists, religious fanatics. In the end they all wind up this way. Self-indulgent frenzy. For kicks, rush, high."

"And society be damned," I added. "After all the know-it-all preaching. Or victim mentality demands."

"Magical thinking."

"Yes, just keep saying it and it'll be true."

"Let reality sink away, all of civilization, into the quicksand of time."

"And then, the Magic Kingdom of everything the way they want it."

She laughed, turned from the window, put her arms around my neck.

"Why don't you just move here? The country, I mean."

"Move? Well, I don't know. I might not get along with some of the people." A sideways nod toward the motorcyclists.

"You don't get along with some people in America."

"That's true." And I thought: Even more there.

We kissed, then moved mutually toward the bed. The motorcycle roar began to fade away. Beneath the covers again, Astrid snuggled against me, a hint of restlessness in her movements.

"I've been wondering a little," she said. "No big deal, but the ethics about what we're doing tomorrow, well, later today now. It's–I mean to say–we're being somewhat deceptive with him, are we not?"

I didn't answer at first. It hadn't bothered me at all, but I had to remember where we were, her country, with the gentle approaches among which she'd grown up. A policeman father would not entirely eclipse the surrounding culture.

"I don't think so," I said. "I think we need to remember the crime, the murder of John, not to mention the details. He's already gotten off easy, way *too* easy, and my plan was formulated in good faith, could even still be tried, theoretically. The fact that it's mostly theoretical isn't something he needs to know. If he's disappointed later, it's a tiny fraction of what he deserves. And he likely killed other people, also horribly. Any deception of him to attain some good is just balancing the scales a little."

Astrid was silent.

"Sorry," I said. "Didn't mean to make a stump speech out of it."

"No, of course you're right."

She took my face in both her hands and kissed me again.

"Tell you what," I said, "maybe when we're done here I can follow through with a letter to his lawyer, pitch the plan to him. He'll no doubt see all the flaws like you did, but we'll be ethically okay. We'll have done our best to use the plan, so no deception."

She seemed to consider for a moment, looking slightly away, but I could tell her mind was wandering.

"Okay," she said softly, and moved in above me.

We obtained our visitor passes without difficulty, Astrid showing her police I.D. and I using my academic "Dr." title. There was a large, well-appointed visitors' lounge for the general population, but we were shown to a stark, separate room for high security prisoners. No other visits were in progress in this room. After some delay, Tapunui was brought down by two guards, one of whom sat down nearby while the other stood by the door. Since ours was the only visitation, the sitting guard would hear much of what was said.

Our subject had a disheveled look, hair and beard grown out since the trial, though not of course to the caveman-like extent I'd witnessed on the farm. He was a large man, and the dull, simmering glower that was his natural expression did not encourage a straightforward approach. Nonetheless, I thought, it was important to remember that we were secure here, guards were at hand, and I had legitimate business with this man, a bone to throw and and to collect on.

Astrid did her best with the awkward introductions, though Tapunui knew me, of course, from the trial. He was no doubt confused as to why one of his enemies should be visiting him. Astrid had anticipated this and prepared visual aids to supplement their shared vocabulary. On a world map she'd drawn an arrow from Kumla to CITED, the Center for Integrative Treatment of Extreme Dysfunction. She'd heavily outlined its state and within this border drawn a circle with slash mark over the word *Död* (death). A notation alongside read *inget dodsstraff* (no death penalty). She pointed at him and me and the map, brought out photos from the Center's website showing the building and myself with the staff, then with clients. Tapunui seemed suspicious but also interested. Astrid moved on with conciliatory gestures between him and myself, segueing into his part of the deal.

"Tell him about my trip," I said to Astrid, "my visit to Rinai's country, the village, her clan."

Conversing was difficult without visual aids. Tapunui glanced at me briefly but showed no other reaction.

"Tell him my friend from the region was killed, but we do not blame him for it."

I heard Astrid use the word for death again and the prisoner was alerted, then took on a guarded expression. The thought of Vic had me wondering what he'd do in my place. I decided he'd take a shot with his own first language, no doubt often heard by Tapunui. I'd learned it myself to a degree in my anthropological studies.

"Ang biyahe ay tungkol kay si Rinai." (The trip was about Rinai.) I pointed to the picture of the Center. "Nariyan siya." (She is there.)

He looked at the picture, did not respond.

"Kinausap ko ang punong. Kasama din si Zel." (I talked with the headman. Also with Zel.)

Tapunui stared at me, said nothing.

"Sinabi niya sa akin ang tungkol kay si Rinai. At tungkol sa mga taong Kakili." (He told me about Rinai. And about the Kakili people."

"Ano ang sinabi niya?" (What did he say?")

I rewarded his speaking with an account of Zel's dismissiveness, his suspicion of Sven, his pointing us to the ziggurat. Tapunui sat stonily, listening without reacting, then looked away.

"Kaya ngayon alam mo na. Ito ang nasa bukid." (So now you know. It was the one at the farm.)

"Pero paano ka naman? Ano ang koneksyon mo?" (But what about you? What is your connection?)

"Lingkod ako. Pinapat ako." (I am a servant. I am summoned.)

"Sino ang tumatawag sa iyo?" (Who summons you?)

"Alam mo. Kasama mo sila." (You know. You have been with them.)

"Sila? Ang kulto ng mga Kakili?" (Them? The cult of the Kakili?)

"Hindi lamang isang kulto. Mga walang hanggang bono." (Not merely a cult. Eternal bonds.

"Anong ibig mong sabihin?" (What do you mean?)

He was silent. I gestured to Astrid for her portfolio, took

out the photos from Frans and Tuva's apartment. There was also a sketch I'd made of the foetal babirusas in their jars. I'd barely laid these out when Tapunui bolted forward, glaring at one or more of the images.

"Siya! Ang gumagawa ng bulok na lahi! Ang bulok na bruha!" (She! The maker of rotten breeds! The rotten witch!)

"Ano yun? Anong ibig mong sabihin?" (What is it? What do you mean?)

"Si Rinai sa bukid na iyon. Lahat ng ginagawa niya. Lahat–" (Rinai on that farm. All her doing. All–)

He lunged at the pictures with a roar and started tearing them to bits. The guard who'd been sitting sprang up and rushed toward us, followed by the guard at the door and then others from the hallway. I held in my hand a modern babirusa tusk, picked up near the ziggurat, which I'd planned to display with the pictures. Tapunui caught sight of it as he struggled with the guards and let out a bellow of new rage. He was eventually subdued and manacled, one of the guards escorting us from the room.

⊛∺϶⊹϶⊱ϵ϶∺⊛

"Did you get anything out of him?" Astrid asked me in the car.

"I'm not sure. He was making some vague references. Tuva might've had something to do with linking Sven up with Rinai."

"Tuva from the antiques store?"

"Right. Except it's just their apartment, they say."

"Hm. Where did you get the new tusk?"

"Vic saw it at the ziggurat. Gave it to me as a joke."

"Poor Vic."

"Yeah. Can't figure that crash. It's like these things keep popping up, unconnected. Except for what we were talking about the other day, the general breakdown of controls, letting

124

something creep or seep through society, the world. The mounting disorder, violence, debasement of humanity."

"Frequency of misfortune with human cause."

"Right. Although the 'human' part makes me wonder."

"Yes, I know. Stop for coffee?"

"Sure."

She parked at an ordinary-looking diner almost empty of customers. A friendly middle-aged waitress took our order for coffees only. Neither of us was hungry.

"I thought," Astrid mused, "it was a 'pen-friend' club that matched Rinai with Sven."

"Just a cover, apparently. Sven or Tuva could have known exactly who they wanted, or one from a very small group, and given extremely narrow specifications. Or they could've skipped the sham search and just paid those people to be go-betweens."

Astrid was reflecting.

"Do we even know there *was* an agency involved?"

"Didn't someone check that out?"

"Not that I'm aware of."

"So maybe then Tuva–"

"Yes, she would be the agency."

The ravings of Tapunui began to make some sense. But then who had he been serving? Who had summoned him? He said I had been with them, but I'd been with many people. The cult of the Kakili was secretive, deceptive, and apparently spreading. The mantle of its destructive power might be worn by any of those who knew of it.

"I think we should get back to Frans and Tuva ASAP," I said, "and this time insist on seeing Tuva. No excuses."

Astrid consulted her "smart phone."

"The last commuter flight has left for today. Weekend schedule. Next one is mid-morning tomorrow. Unless you want to drive all the way, barge in on Saturday night."

"No, that's all right. We'll be Sunday visitors."

Back in our hotel room, Astrid indulged in a long bath while I checked my email. I saw there was a message from Midori and opened it first. Direct as always, my colleague informed me that I was no longer a charter member at the Center or, of course, its assistant director. The vote had been four to one with one abstention, Midori my lone supporter while Rachel wanted no part. My status was now that of a provisional employee with no assigned duties, more or less on a par with the aides. The Center's credit card account that I'd been using had been cancelled. It appeared Bart would be the new assistant director, though Rudy had succeeded in delaying this decision. Midori said she wanted to meet with me before I showed up at the Center, that she strongly looked forward to my return. She did not request I call, did not express any judgment of our colleagues. I looked up from the message and heard Astrid softly singing in the bath, caught a whiff of her steam, reflected on how maybe I'd gone too far in some way.

There was another message that commanded my attention. It was from the Capt. Edward who'd accosted me in the Sea Breeze Hotel. He wanted me to know that he'd successfully contacted Vic's family through his employer, enabling the proper shipment of Vic's body and belongings. He also thought I'd be interested to know there was a large explosion in the autonomous zone the day after my departure. It had destroyed an ancient tower or temple called a ziggurat, as well as filled or plugged a deep pit or tunnel beneath it, a feature of much local conjecture. The explosion raised an overpowering stench that spread throughout the kingdom, stronger and more nauseating than anything the people had experienced.

I logged off, returned Astrid's phone to her pile of belongings. I sat in an upholstered chair, legs extended, head back on the cushioned top edge. I closed my eyes and tried to clear my mind, succeeding only in replacing thoughts of the present with fragments from the past. The frugality in childhood, the animosity in the community, cruelty and violence as bases of power, a heinous crime unsolved. Fear, always fear. The attempt to adjust but meeting only deception, crudity, and again scenes of violence. The weakness of institutions, fragile structures easily blown to bits like an old temple in the jungle. And the self, finally the self, in league with what it seeks to destroy, drawing power from what it sees deep in the murderous eyes of a cobra.

"So are you hungry now, Mr. Investigator?"

Astrid's voice, far away, but I instinctively brought her closer.

"Shall we go out or are you too tired? Shall we see about getting delivery?"

My eyes had opened and were adjusting, saw her in terrycloth robe and towel turban, standing before the mirror.

"No, I'm fine," I said. "Let's go out, take the air."

"I saw pizza and sushi places down the street, or would you prefer something blander? Hello, are you with me?"

"What? Yes, I'm with you. Sure, bland is fine."

She gave me a quick look, then returned to the mirror, undid the towel turban and tended to her hair. I wondered briefly where she'd gotten the robe, then noticed that the terrycloth was thin and cheap so it was no doubt hotel issue. My inquisitive mind, I reflected, would it be the death of me? Perhaps, if I didn't choose my actions wisely. But the next day's return to Frans and Tuva was scheduled in stone, beyond which we would see. I wouldn't be conceding to the demons just yet, no matter what they thought of me at CITED.

⊷⊷⊱⊱⊹⊱⊰⊰⊶⊶

Back in Malmo the following day, we arrived at Frans

and Tuva's building in early afternoon. Astrid parked her car behind a moving truck planted squarely in front of the entrance doors. We were not concerned this time about being seen. Entering the lobby, we saw that the door to the stairway was propped open, probably by the movers, saving us the need to ring the apartment's bell and be buzzed in. We climbed the stairs, prepared to aggressively knock on the couple's door, but found that it, too, was propped open, the voices of young adult males issuing from within. We entered and found them sweeping and picking up nondescript trash, all that remained of the exotic display I'd so recently scrutinized.

"What's going on here?" I inquired.

"We're just finishing up," said the closer workman. "The other truck has already left."

"Back for a last look?" called the man farther back.

Astrid explained that we were not the tenants, or ex-tenants, simply customers come to buy items we'd seen there before. We'd had no idea the other couple was moving. Could the workers please give us the new address?

"The stuff's going to a warehouse," said the first workman, "up in Sundsvall." And he fished out a work order.

"Where's that?" I asked Astrid.

"Well north of the capital, five or six hundred kilometers. A port on the Gulf of Bothnia."

She stepped forward to jot the address on the small pad she always carried. It was clear enough to me, however, that Frans and Tuva had eluded us. Aside from the promised letter to Tapunui's lawyer, I had no further business in this country for now. None, at least, that could retain priority over the attention I owed to my professional crisis at the Center.

VIII.

There were few passengers in business class on my flight back to America. This made one of them more noticeable to me, a turbaned man one row up and off to the right. I couldn't be sure at first, but I suspected I'd seen him on this route before, when Astrid and I transported Rinai. My suspicion was confirmed when, shortly into the flight, he rose from his seat and turned to pass me toward the restrooms.

"Hello," he said. "We've flown together before, have we not?"

"Yes, I believe we have. December?"

"Exactly. My name is Patel." And he offered his hand.

I gave him the Gaelic version of my first name, shook the hand.

"Are the two ladies with you?" He looked around.

"No, not this trip."

"Ah, too bad. The lonely traveler, eh? But I'm always alone when I travel. Safety engineer for the oil interests."

"You had oil business in Sweden?"

He laughed.

"No, I stop there for the pure cold air, to get the desert and oil fumes out of my lungs. And you, may I ask what is your business?"

"I'm a therapist. People with emotional difficulties."

"Ah. And that requires international travel?"

"At times, yes."

"Hm. Tell me, do you by any chance play chess?"

"I know the moves, but I haven't played for quite some time."

"I'm sure you're being modest. I have a small set with me. We'll play when I get back." And he continued on his way to a business class restroom.

I soon discovered that he was an atrocious player, or at least seemed to be. I declined to take advantage of his shoddy moves, extending the game out of courtesy, but had to win to avoid being obvious. We played all the way to checkmate, he never seeing the closing combination. In our second game, I deliberately blundered into a checkmate trap, trying to give him a win, but he missed the opportunity. I had to blunder again into a queen-for-knight exchange, allowing me to reasonably concede shortly after. Inwardly chafed by the low level of play, I quickly dispatched him in the rubber match, decisively ending the series.

"A therapist," he said as we sipped our cocktails. "But tell me, do you really think you change them, the disturbed ones? I mean deep down, permanently. Not just for the present."

"Well, of course there are limits. Problems of recent origin are much more treatable than those long entrenched, possibly a component of the subject's character or even his basic nature."

"So what do you do then?"

"The main focus for a deep-set problem has to be pragmatic, enabling the subject to function normally in his day-to-day interactions."

Patel nodded, sipping his drink reflectively.

"Are there any you cannot reach at all? Violent ones?"

Almost immediately, Tapunui came to mind. Without giving names or exact locations, I put his story forth as an example.

"He was one," I concluded, "that I would have to say was beyond the pale."

"Yes, obviously. A shame he won't be executed. Perhaps karma will come through. But, you know, that weakness in institutions is rampant nowadays. The courts, government bureaus, and such are ill-equipped to deal with even moderate cases of *pure evil*, much less the severe or extreme cases met by men like us. My own work also has its moments."

"Safety engineer?"

"It's not simply checking for loose bolts on the rigs."

I took a sip, waiting for him to elaborate.

"One must be alert at all times. Not only to obvious, moronic criminal types, but also to masters of deception and their acolytes. They may infiltrate an organization or group of any kind, usurp its purpose, make destruction or plunder seem noble. Or they might act out of sinister ambition, operating alone or perhaps with stooges. Even the seemingly altruistic are not to be trusted, some of them are the worst. But forgive me, I should not burden you with my cynicism."

"No, I wholly sympathize. I only wonder about personal relationships, especially the most intimate. When does such an approach allow trust to begin?"

"Some would say never, but I'm not quite among them. We all must eventually trust someone or else kill ourselves or go crazy."

"And thus, the better option: simple alertness."

"A healthy cynicism, yes. Strong skepticism."

"Short of paranoia, of course."

"I should hope so."

We soon joined most of the other passengers in sleeping away the hours, lights dimmed. Upon arrival, we accompanied each other through security and baggage retrieval. Our episode of camaraderie drawing to a close, Patel requested contact information, so I gave him a phone number I reserve for brush-offs, that of an inner-city pizzeria. I felt no compunction in this since I believed he'd given me a phony name. We therefore parted as anonymous strangers, the same as before our meeting.

I felt in need of rest when I reached my apartment, the socializing with Patel having shortened my in-flight sleep. I was alert enough, however, to detect subtle changes in my accustomed surroundings. I could think of no reason why a water glass should be sitting on the end table next to my recliner, nor why the back support cushion should be moved to another chair, sitting crookedly as if flipped. I recalled a similar situation in my office on New Year's Day, when I'd stopped by the Center unexpectedly. Rinai had been in a bad mood that day. Some books had been out of order then so I now checked my shelves and–yes, they were replaced unevenly and with a novel stuck among reference books. I sniffed the air for an unusual scent but did not detect one, though there'd been plenty of time for one to dissipate.

I made my way to the bedroom. There was a slight impression on the bedspread, its size suggesting a small person, and the spread was pulled up rather sloppily over one of the pillows. I took a moment to question myself about who might have a key. I hadn't given one to Midori, or to anyone else, and this wasn't the work of maintenance, who anyway always left a note. A burglar would've stolen something and probably trashed the place. I wondered what the intruder had been looking for, if anything. Perhaps he or she–I guessed she–had simply wanted to share my space for a while.

I lay in the impression left on my bed, fell asleep, dreamed of nothing. I woke to failing daylight through the blinds, remembered that I should call Midori.

"I'm back," I greeted her on the phone.

"Good. Don't come here. Meet me at that cheap steakhouse near the tennis club."

"You mean the birthplace of our blossoming romance?"

"You got it. I'm out of here in an hour."

"Okay, fine."

She hung up. I stared at my phone a moment, then clicked off. I guessed that I was missing something, maybe a lot.

The temperature outside, I assumed, would be dropping precipitously. The winter had been unusually cold, though snowfall was normal. Entering the walk-in to fetch a sweater, I saw that things were somewhat jumbled, again unlike my personal order. I grabbed the first sweater I saw and turned away irritated.

Midori had already taken a table when I arrived at the steakhouse. It was a darker sort of place, the table candles being more a necessity than a decoration.

"I take it you got my email," she said. "The vote, your new status and all."

"Yeah, I did. Sorry I didn't keep in touch better. A lot came up after we last talked. My friend Vic was killed in a crash that same night."

"Oh, I'm sorry. That must have been really bad for you."

I gave her the details, placing the event in context with our search for the Kakili, the destruction of the ziggurat. Midori was content to listen, prompting me to move on with my return to Scania, Tuva's collection, the episode at the Kumla prison. There was no avoiding mention of Astrid, central as she was to my efforts, though I referred to her as "Detective Ulrickson."

"When I got back to my apartment here," I concluded, "I found I'd had a visitor. He or she had sat in the recliner perusing my books, beverage on end table. Gone in and lay on the bed awhile, rummaged in the closet."

"Did you notice anything missing?"

"Not yet. I haven't completely checked."

"You have a blue wool shirt, don't you? Dark blue, herringbone pattern?"

"Yes. What about it?"

"Rinai was wearing it one morning at the Center. Early, just after getting up. I thought I'd seen it when I was over."

"Ah."

"I won't venture an interpretation."

"Nor will I."

"She'd been out by herself the previous afternoon."

"I see."

"The fact is, she feels free to come and go from the Center as she pleases. Rachel has very little influence on her. The pattern is enabled by a breakdown of structure in our facility. How can there be protocol for intense therapy when you have part-time eating disorders and split personalities walking around? He even admitted a reincarnation. Not even original, an Egyptian princess."

"Dr. Gruner?"

"Yes. Though he has the dynamic duo–Bart and Rudy– each bending an ear. They're still contending for your job, your old position I mean."

"Funny I haven't been officially notified on that. The credit card I noticed on my own, it just stopped working."

"Like I say, it's gotten really slipshod there. You might want to meet with Gruner straight away when you arrive. Negotiate something, avoid the jackals."

"I'll do that. And thanks for toughing it out for me, Midori. On that vote nonsense and with Rinai."

"What can I say? I missed you and–" Her voice trailed off.

"It's good to be back," I said.

⚏⚏⚏

I let the workday start without me, had a leisurely breakfast at a fast-food restaurant, circled the Center in my car and watched it from a distance before approaching. I saw Rudy leading a group in slow-motion exercises out on the grounds, their motions inhibited by layers of thick clothing against the cold. The dog-walking man who'd spoken with me watched from afar. Here and there an insouciant figure slumped, moping along or smoking, whether client or staff I could not tell.

I parked in the lot and approached the building, a male addict cheerily greeting me. In the lobby were the guards, several clients, and Helen, chatting with a woman in what looked like a century-old wedding dress. I casually strode through in the direction of Dr. Gruner's office.

"How was vacation?" called a guard.

"Great!" I waved back.

The director's door was ajar and male voices issued from within. I discreetly entered and found Bart standing before Gruner's desk, arms folded and confident. Awkward greetings were exchanged and the would-be assistant excused himself, Gruner making no effort to detain him. I was gestured to a chair, the director's expression one of cautious bemusement.

"You had us wondering."

"A lot happened."

"Indeed."

"I apologize for the lack of communication."

"Well, that's done with now. You're here, communicating."

"There were substantial developments in the Rinai study."

"Oh?"

I launched into an account of Tapunui's trial and its results, my persistence with Frans and Tuva, the disastrous hunt for the Kakili. I omitted any reference to Astrid or the seemingly irrelevant Patel. It sounded now like a song of futility, yet Gruner listened with noticeably increasing interest. As I closed he nodded sagely.

"Exactly why I hired you," he said.

"Sir?"

"That investigative nature, physical persistence, taking the hits as they come. A welcome complement to us armchair types."

I ventured a slight smile, savoring the word "welcome."

"Unfortunately, a divergent approach can sometimes tax an operation, bring about misunderstanding, resentment."

I was silent.

"You've heard about the vote that was taken?"

"I have, yes."

"Regrettable, I know, but a critical mass of opinion among people I need, as well as a majority of charter members. But I'm sure we can work it out, you and I, to nullify any negative effects on your status here or your career."

A blank slate appeared in my thoughts. Midori had been right about negotiating.

"What did you have in mind, sir?"

"Well, it's occurred to me that, while we're a 24-hour operation, our professional and management activity is basically on office hours. I could use a night manager to come in around three or four in the afternoon and hold the fort up to eleven or midnight. The matron can still cover sleepy time. You'd also function as community liaison. We were going to have Helen do that, you'll recall, but I think it'd cut into her therapist duties too much. The new position will get you a twenty percent increase in pay. Plus, you can make the call on your successor as A.D., the choice being Bart or Rudy."

I relaxed in my chair, mostly pleased but wary of the closing detail. It was obviously something he wanted to dump.

"If I may make a suggestion, sir, why not split our service staff into two parts, or units, and make Bart and Rudy each a team leader over one unit. You could then simply assign an incoming case to one or the other unit and the team leader would be responsible for assigning a worker. It'd make things easier for you and provide a pyramidal structure for the Center."

Dr. Gruner sat back himself now. I had a feeling that he'd have said "done" in our pre-vote days.

"Not a bad idea," he contented himself with responding. "Did you have any other suggestions?"

"Well, you might obtain a receptionist. Multitasking in the lobby seems rather much for the guards."

❦

I was pleasantly surprised by the new arrangement. It was much better than I'd hoped for, even with minimal "negotiating." I thought I might have gone too far in suggesting Bart and Rudy as "team leaders" rather than supervisors, but Gruner kept the designation, thus indicating they were still to carry cases. My assigned hours I found to be a trade-off, freeing me from the daytime folderol but cancelling most of my evenings with Midori. She was supportive, though, when I expressed my regret to her.

"Never mind," she said. "We still have the late-night hours. They're the most important, after all."

I didn't argue, of course, though I'd be missing our wine-assisted conversations over dinner. I thought of them as I began my new duties the day after receiving them. It led me to reflect on the future relationship of Midori and myself, its degree of exclusiveness, expectations we might share or not share. Questions would arise, answers might be difficult. My meetings with Astrid were quite recent and implicitly ongoing, though the distance between us seemed prohibitive. Perhaps my new working hours would help in this, slowing discussion of the future, allowing things to work themselves out. I could then sit here peacefully in the evenings with my peccadilloes on hold.

The first night I mostly got my footing, making the rounds

and getting used to seeing the clients and guards within the new time frame. The workers had mostly lost their enthusiasm for staying late, even Rudy only hanging around an extra hour or so. The night matron came on at nine, so for several hours I was a manager with no staff, the guards working for an outside contractor. I noticed, perhaps because staff was absent, that the Center was rather heavy with resident clients. On checking our roster, I found that, while we showed a steady influx of clients, there was only one discharge (the shoplifting state official, supposedly cured) and one pending transfer (the psychosomatic stiff-arm, admitted in error). We were not building much of a track record, though a breakthrough on Rinai could change everything, give Gruner and the Center celebrity status.

"How did it go?" Midori asked later.

"Quiet, mostly. The clients behaved themselves, maybe wary of me."

"Just wait."

We were in her apartment, the bedroom, in near-darkness. Due to the intrusion at my place, we'd agreed she shouldn't be there alone.

"By the way," I said, "these excursions of Rinai, has anyone discovered a basic reason for them? Rachel, by some chance, in her work, or Dr. Gruner in analysis?"

"Rachel's completely at sea with her. Gruner took one shot at analysis, said Rinai was uncooperative. But then, he's only done one other analysis since we opened. Snake-boy."

"It was supposed to be part of the treatment protocol."

"I guess many are called, few are chosen."

She was still speaking as she rolled toward me under the covers. Discussion over, the late hour asserted itself, breathlessly.

With my second and third evenings as night manager, the novelty wore off and I sensed a certain tawdriness in the Center's activity. The guards seemed less resolute, less alert, than they were when Sgt. Hendon was on duty. With only the corporal supervising, they often strayed from their posts or patrol routes, increasing their smoke breaks in the lunchroom or outside, and fraternizing with clients. Some of the clients emulated them, giving vent to their crudest and rudest impulses, drawing laughter or angry retorts. Things would subside when I made myself visible, but chaos would close behind me as I passed.

Except for Rinai, I saw little reason to attend to the clients. I had no duties specifically mine except the community liaison role. I therefore spent time speculating on how best to educate our host suburb and others on the value of our institution. Not being familiar with the media or public speaking formats, I stuck to making general notes at first. The idea, as I saw it, was to make us look good, to put people like the dog-walking man at ease when they saw strange things happening on our grounds, or if they happened to meet one of our clients who'd wandered away. On a larger scale, there was our tax-exempt status to think of, our endowments, our eligibility for government assistance. I needed to stress the uniqueness and relevance of our services, the expertise of our staff, their dedication and selflessness, the quality of our facilities, the vision and nobility of our leader. With a few photos, mostly of our grounds and exterior, plus a studio portrait of Gruner, we'd have a decent brochure for general use. Any speaking engagements could simply amplify the brochure content.

While I was occupied with this project on my fourth night, Cpl. Colyer came in and informed me that Rinai had left the Center unaccompanied. He was apparently ceding responsibility to me in case something bad happened. We knew Rinai had done this before, and she was within her rights legally, but the residents were under a covenant that required permission from their workers.

"Did she have a statement from Rachel?"

"No, sir. Just waltzed right through."

"All right, corporal. I'll follow up."

As my shift wore on, I received an unexpected call from Midori. She was at my apartment since there'd been no further intrusions since my return. There had just been an attempt, however, while Midori was relaxing in the living room.

"I heard a noise by the door and thought it was you, home early for some reason. The chain was on so I got up to take it off. I heard it clunk as it stopped the door opening, thought it funny you didn't call out. I peeked through the opening but didn't see anyone. I listened but everything was quiet."

"Are you okay?"

"Yeah, I guess. Think I should call the police?"

"Well, is there any damage to the door or lock?"

"No, they must have picked it."

"Right. Let's hold off on the police. Unless the person comes back, of course. I have an idea what happened. Don't go to bed until I get there."

"Of course I won't."

My work on the liaison project was still laid out before me, but it had dropped precipitously in importance. I was conscious of something concerning me that was evolving in Rinai's mind, affecting her actions, attracting notice from others. I imagined the blue herringbone shirt and her wearing it. Was there a fixation of some sort developing? I could easily enough confront her on the matter, cut off the process before it got out of control. It would be a normal, professional thing to do, maybe even therapeutically sound. But I would lose the psychological advantage of silence, letting things ride as she and the truth revealed themselves. I was primarily an investigator, after all.

My shift passed. I sat in my office, waiting for something more to happen. Nothing did. I departed with vague misgivings.

"You didn't check on her before you left?" Midori asked at the apartment. She was wearing her lightly quilted robe.

"No. Cpl. Colyer will know when she came in. Maybe also the night matron."

"She's getting to be rather much, isn't she?"

"She always was. That's why we have her at the Center, why she's key to its success."

"Can we please go to bed?" Midori sighed.

⋯⊰⊱⋯

We slept late in the morning, having forgotten to set the alarm with the night's distraction. Midori moved swiftly in the new daylight, preparing for work while I, the night man, watched from the bed. I saw that she'd be quickly out the door so we wouldn't have breakfast together this day. Another sacrifice to my new schedule, albeit unforeseen. I arose and donned my robe to at least kiss her goodbye.

"Three, three-thirty then?" she asked.

"Thereabouts. Can you check on Rinai if you get the chance?"

"Will do."

And with that she was off, leaving me to ponder anew the connections between my job, my broader purpose, Midori, and now Rinai's odd intrusions. I couldn't get around the idea that, if there was a way forward toward the ultimate source of evil, it was through Rinai's private world. I was somewhat disappointed with Rachel, and more so with Dr. Gruner, for providing so little in terms of insight. If I were to get anywhere, it seemed I had to involve myself more directly with Rinai, perhaps by turning my night shift assignment to my advantage. That would certainly be payback for my lost time with Midori.

I was still musing on this over breakfast when the telephone rang. It was Midori, confused noises in the background.

"Something's happened. Big time. Really terrible."

"What is it, Midori?"

"Amelia hung herself. Helen's client, back in her room. Police are all over the place. It's chaos."

I was stunned, fought against it.

"Okay, try to relax. Get off to the side somewhere. I'll just get dressed and then I'm on my way."

"Okay."

My mind, so recently engaged in calm reasoning and attempts at planning, was now a swirling storm as I yielded to reflexive action and anger. As if things weren't difficult enough, I thought, more has to be piled on. And on and on. But I had no one to blame it all on, no single agent, and this was frustrating. Amelia had killed her own children; suicide was always a likelihood. We had tried to prevent it, but she was the agent of her own death. Not us, and certainly not some omnipotent source of evil, some Kakili. Though the word gave me pause, somehow. I was too preoccupied, too confused, to analyze anything at the moment, but I ordered myself to get back to it later, to determine where this, like all evil, fit into the scheme of things.

On approaching the Center, I saw that the parking lot was dominated by emergency response vehicles, including vans from a couple of TV stations. There could be no effective coverup by Dr. Gruner. I parked out on the street and slogged through slushy snow to the building. It was a sunny morning, not quite freezing, a break in the weather that felt inappropriate for this day. There was no attempt by police to block the doors, occupied as they were within, but I found Sgt. Hendon of the guards standing stalwart in the lobby, mostly being ignored by news crews and others milling about.

"Have you seen Dr. Tateyama?" I asked him.

"She's back there with the coroner, where it happened. They know each other from the other time."

"Oh yes, I recall. By the way, did Cpl. Colyer pass anything along to you? Anything I should know about last night?"

"No, sir. He high-tailed it out before the worker found the body. These boys'll be paying him a visit later, I expect."

"You say a worker discovered the scene. Would that be Helen?"

"Yes, sir. And she's mighty, mighty upset. I'd be real careful with her. Gentle-like."

"Of course. Thank you, sergeant."

I decided to seek out Midori before meeting with my other colleagues. I passed without comment through support staff, guards, and reporters, my new I.D. in hand for police blocking access. Night manager, the one who was in charge, they'd no doubt think. I passed Rinai's room, no one in it but the bed looking slept in. Amelia's room was next door. Police and various technicians were standing about, one with a camera, the body lying on the floor on the far side of the bed. A thin rope or cord suspended from overhead pipes had been cut and dangled above the body. I did not at first see a chair or anything the deceased might have been standing on, but then noticed a portable three-step staircase that had apparently been moved to make room for the body. The coroner and Midori were standing before it, comparing notes, when she happened to look up and see me. She excused herself and came over.

"Thanks for coming," she said. "The others have been useless. Mostly huddled in Gruner's office."

"Any details yet on what happened? Why she did it just now, a time frame by hours, her exact procedure?"

"He's not sure he'll call it suicide. The detectives are pointing out the drapery cord came from the library, as did the wooden steps. Also, her room was supposed to be locked."

I took a moment to absorb this.

"What about the time frame?"

"He wanted between midnight and three a.m. I pushed for something later. He settled on one to four."

I almost thanked her. Any distance, any mitigation of my own culpability was precious. Then I noticed the coroner looking over, two attendants raising the now covered body onto a gurney.

"I guess he wants to finish up."

"Okay," Midori said. "See you later. Love you."

She hastened away. I eased through the somber public servants and out of the room, passing Rinai's again. It occurred to me that I hadn't asked Midori about her. But then, she would have been preoccupied with the death since she arrived. I could look for Rinai myself or at least talk with Rachel, but I should first check in with Dr. Gruner, offer to make myself useful in the crisis, absolve myself of any blame. I headed purposefully toward his office, somewhat dazed by it all but noticing Rudy talking to reporters. Yes, I thought, that's in character, something natural to be happening.

I found Gruner's door closed but not locked, presumed to look in without knocking, saw him at his desk with Bart and Helen in two chairs before him, close together. Other chairs had been pulled up but were empty now.

"Come in," Gruner said flatly.

I advanced and took a seat on one side of his desk. Bart and Helen gave me resentful looks, she with reddened eyes. Bart had been miffed by my night manager assignment, his concomitant appointment as team leader instead of assistant director. Helen's expression, I sensed, was mostly of more immediate origin. There was an awkward silence, Dr. Gruner sitting passively instead of offering a talking point. I'd anticipated he would thank me for coming in, as Midori had, it being long before my new starting time.

"What's the matter with you?" Helen blurted. "How could you let it happen?"

I was silent, waiting for one of the others to intervene. Neither did. Bart exuded sanctimonious support.

"Don't you understand fragility in a person?" Helen continued. "How you have to be competent *at all times*? That was a crime! A *crime*!"

Bart laid his hand on her arm. Dr. Gruner finally stirred.

"Bart, I think maybe–" He nodded and gestured toward the door. "Perhaps the chapel."

Bart led his wife out, giving me a dour glance on the way.

"A crime!" Helen shouted again at the door.

Dr. Gruner and I sat still a few moments, allowing the charged atmosphere to regain stasis.

"She's probably right," I said, "about a crime being committed."

The director looked at me in surprise, uncomprehending. I then gave him a third-hand account of the detectives' findings, to be incorporated in the coroner's report with implications far exceeding Helen's estimation of my competence. Dr. Gruner listened with interest, then with anxiety and worry.

"So she was assisted, maybe murdered, by someone in the Center?"

"I'm afraid so."

"It couldn't be a worker, of course."

"I agree. And a guard is highly unlikely."

"So then, a client. And the question becomes, what do we do about it?"

"If I may suggest, sir, I think you should immediately reassign the case of Rinai to myself. I have reason to believe she's connected with this and information from from abroad I can use to work with her. Success with her case will reverse today's damage, prove we can handle even the most extreme dysfunction."

He considered for a moment, but there was no other way.

"Do you want Rachel to assist you?"

"No, sir. I'd want Megan the aide. A fresh start. Rachel can be given the community liaison role."

IX.

The Center was closed for two days to all except residents, staff, and guards. As the police finished their initial investigation, normal operations were permitted to resume, but normality was of course impossible. Arriving in mid-afternoon, I'd enter an atmosphere drained of optimism and positive emotion, suffused instead with fear and amorphous guilt. It had become well known that Amelia had not been the lone actor in her death. A cloud of suspicion therefore loomed, along with the inevitable self-questioning–could I or we have done something, or something more, to prevent etc., etc. Some may have seen the Center as doomed, even considered quitting, but I along with Gruner knew our strongest card was still in play.

"Have you heard anything?" Rudy asked me in the hall. "Do they suspect anyone yet?"

"I don't know any more than you do," I told him.

"But they talk to you a lot, being night manager and all."

"Listen. If they don't talk to you much, it's good. It means you're not a suspect."

"But what about Luke?" he asked, referring to snake-boy, his star client. "One of them took quite an interest."

"I'm sure they saw he's not smart enough to pull it off. Just keep his door locked and he won't get in trouble,"

"Yeah, the locks. They haven't been so dependable lately."

I couldn't argue with him on that. I told him I had work to do, which was truer than he could know, and proceeded to my office.

Rachel had furnished me with her case file on Rinai, while I'd given her my plans as community liaison. Sitting at my desk with my colleague's notes, I found they were written in the tentative, non-judgmental style of a college textbook. Family and community characteristics were continually the foci of conversations with Rinai. She'd come from a rather large brood, unclear just *how* big since parenting was collective among the village women, the men claiming only some children they favored. The village was basically a degenerate commune, I interpreted, almost entirely dependent on governments and charities. Rachel described the sporadic education received from young, swiftly disenchanted visiting teachers. She also described games and dances, customs and traditional dishes. Rinai had mentioned ceremonies related to typhoons, earthquakes, disease outbreaks and such, but not much detail was provided. "There were sacrifices," she'd said, but had not elaborated on the point.

I relegated Rachel's case file to the bottom drawer of my desk, replaced it with a clean pad of paper, took pen in hand. I began writing names and phrases at different points on the sheet, connecting them with lines, tried to create a web of meaning, of truth.

The starting point for me had been John, his telling me about Sven and Rinai, but the actual starting point had been well before that. One could say it was when Sven's father died and the son became lonely, or when his great-grandmother gave him the ancient babirusa tusk, or when Tuva entered the picture and facilitated Sven's union with Rinai. One could choose from many points, dating all the way back to the misty origins of humanity. But from where I sat, the problem I faced began when the Kakili was introduced into Scania,

147

either by Sven or Rinai. She blamed Sven, but the evidence suggested it was Rinai herself. She was the one who was into sacrifices. If she hadn't foreseen what might happen, if the force sometimes could not be controlled, it didn't matter. She was still accountable.

Rinai's small fires in the farmland were apparently part of an appeal to the Kakili, answered eventually by the materialization of Tapunui, rational explanation pending. Drawn to Sven's farm, the henchman mistakenly destroyed the chicken coop, or else he was issuing a warning as Rinai's mother had predicted. He then successively murdered Sven, the laborer from the adjoining farm, and John. Sven might have been an intended victim, the other two gratuitous for lack of direction from Rinai. The man on the plane was her own work, motive unclear, perhaps a botched attempt against me or Astrid, method to be clarified. The female guard was found between Rinai's window and Amelia's, killed by Tapunui's method, perhaps another mistake as Rinai sacrificed in her room. The man in the motel must have aroused Rinai's anger, as I myself did when she found Midori at my apartment, Amelia innocently paying the price. Vic's death, a purported accident, was nonetheless in Rinai's home country, Kakili territory, where we were snooping. Alarms and demands for retribution would travel swiftly in a telepathic cult.

I contemplated my jottings and connections on the pad. There clearly was a randomness in events, even where design was intended. One could generalize and say there is randomness in evil and so it is uncontrollable, even by itself. But the fact that human actions are always, to some extent, by design means there are centers of power and planning that can be attacked to expunge a great amount of evil. Even crimes that seem random, "mistakes" by lesser figures, often derive from empowerment by a stronger source. Unlike vicious animals, disease, or bad luck, injuries by human agents are always deliberate, an abuse of cognitive ability. The conceivers must therefore be rooted out and neutralized, not deserving mercy since they know what they are doing.

I brought in Megan to discuss our approach to Rinai. She wore a green velvet band holding back her light brown hair. I complemented her on it and she relaxed.

"Are you familiar with telekinesis?" I asked.

She looked at me a moment, then relaxed again.

"That would be *para*psychology. It came up a couple of times in my courses, mostly as an example of pseudoscience."

"Yes, that's understandable. We do want to be rational. With this case, however, we have holes in our knowledge of methods and motives. We may have to briefly consider, ah, remote possibilities."

Her youthful face betrayed a guilty interest. I pressed on.

"Maybe I should be more specific. Beyond telekinesis there's teleportation, the old sci-fi staple. And then, in the more exotic realms of belief, there's bilocation. I don't think we'll have to deal with that one, however."

"We'll stop at teleportation."

"Yes. You may remember, when we talked with Rinai before, I showed her the old animal tusk and she spoke of its having power, a power that dated back to her and Sven's remote ancestors, prehistoric. It appears that the power, if it exists, does not originate in the tusk but in an entity called the Kakili, to which Rinai and others have been offering sacrifices."

"Sacrifices?"

"Yes, possibly including human. To perform some of them, or for vengeance or other reasons, Rinai supposedly summons fellow cult members, 'servants of the Kakili,' through telepathy and teleportation. That's *mental* teleporting, mind over matter."

"Wow. She has that power over them?"

"There's probably some kind of pecking order. Maybe not, but that would get into bilocation–'Here, borrow my second self.' Doubtful, I'd say. Doesn't even fit well in quantum physics."

"So we'll just stay with teleportation."

"Right. I hope this isn't too crazy for you."

"Hey, I'm game! Really, I can hardly wait."

"Good."

I wondered later if I'd laid it on too thick with Megan. I'd wanted to prepare her for our session with Rinai, with whom she'd been a help the other time. I assumed that, with her youthfulness, she'd be resilient to whatever I said, accepting rather than skeptical. But I hadn't considered the enthusiasm that youth also engenders. The business with Rinai was of utmost importance. We mustn't be led down the path to dances and traditional dishes, as Rachel had. Megan should sit mostly as witness, I thought, while I controlled the interview.

There was an email from Astrid requesting that I call. We hadn't been in contact since my return to America. Since it was the middle of the night in Scania, I resolved to call the next day from home. It occurred to me that, with all that had happened here since my return, Astrid was aware of none of it. I reflected on the value, indeed the necessity, of propinquity in a relationship. Without it other people, events, issues grabbed the higher rungs of priority and a valued connection was weakened, became remote, trivial, or was lost.

When I called after breakfast I had trouble getting through, it being the work day on both ends. When I finally heard Astrid speak, it was over a background of police activity.

"Sounds pretty busy there."

"There's been an uptick in street crime. Feeds the immigration issue, so pressure gets applied."

"Hope you're not working too hard."

"Oh, I'm still sane. So far. How about you?"

"Well, speaking of issues, pressure, I'm somewhat in the eye of a storm."

I described the happenings since my return, avoiding mention of Midori but with inescapable emphasis on the "suicide."

"Right there in your building? What a shock it had to be!"

"Yes. Her worker is still quite shaken. Normally a calm, deliberative person."

"Was Rinai around when it happened?"

The question took me by surprise, Astrid quick to make connection.

"Actually, that's unclear at the moment."

"Oh, I see."

"I'll be talking with her tomorrow, find out what she knows about Tapunui."

"Good idea. Many missing details on that. He's been deported, by the way."

"It actually went through?"

"Yes, finally. They went the payment route."

"Who took him?"

"You were just there yourself."

"Not Rinai's country?"

"They underbid a nicer place, remote South Pacific."

"Guess the king really needs the money."

"There was also some kind of politics involved."

"Hm. The A-Zone, or maybe the Kakili influence."

"Good you're out of there, anyway."

"Definitely. Any information on Frans and Tuva?"

"Yes, sort of. We checked out the address that the movers gave you, up in Sundsvall. It is in fact a warehouse and some of their stuff is still there. There was a later order to ship certain units to a warehouse in Africa, Mozambique. Frans and Tuva apparently have connections there. They flew there shortly after we visited them, per airline records."

"Did you inspect the items still in Sundsvall?"

"Most were in boxes and crates. I recognized the big drum, a couple of rolled-up tapestries, but we couldn't open containers without a warrant, per the warehouse manager, and we lacked enough probable cause to get one."

"Were any of the containers marked *Fragile*? As if they maybe contained jars of liquid with baby pigs?"

"No, nothing like that."

"You were there personally?"

"Yes."

"Who was with you? The local police?"

"Yes, and Nils."

"Nils made the trip? I'm surprised."

"Well, he recognized the address of the warehouse. It's the place where they arrested Tapunui."

"He'd been hiding there?"

"Apparently."

"And you still had no probable cause on the boxes?"

"Nothing real concrete, solid enough for a judge."

"Harboring a fugitive?"

"Well, all we had with the boxes were your suspicions, your theories. Some of which–let's face it–were pretty well 'out there.'"

"Out there?"

"Yes. I mean, I could buy into them myself but–well, I was swept up by you, Mr. Investigator. So I was more receptive to your thinking than others would be."

"Oh. Okay. But then Nils went with you to Sundsvall."

"Yes, I talked him into it. He accommodated me. Then *he* was accommodated by the local police."

"Accommodation. Yes, it's good that we do that for each other."

━━◦┠◦┨◦┠◦━━

I came away from the call to Astrid with mixed feelings. I was gratified that she'd been to the warehouse in Sundsvall, that the whereabouts of Frans and Tuva had been discovered, but the dispositions on the situation rang rather hollow. Tapunui, the killer of John and probably others, had been freed into a land where he could find friends and support, enabled to do further harm either on his own behalf or as a tool of others. The investigation of his link to Tuva had ended with the assumption that a warrant could not be obtained. However true this was, at least an attempt could have been made, the probable cause perhaps enhanced a bit to sway the judge. I wondered if this might be another instance of timorousness in the national culture. There was also apparently no consideration of extraditing Frans and Tuva from Mozambique. It was almost as if, once people were out of the country, their crimes and even criminal networks were "out of sight, out of mind."

But I was also disturbed on another, more personal level, the reasons less clear but still compelling. I had sensed an undefinable difference in the emotional tone and cadence of Astrid's voice, a shade less intimacy, perhaps more than a shade. The "out there" remark seemed out of character, caught me off guard. I realized she'd been at work, caught up in things there, but in my experience people had a way of guarding their connections with those they most cared about. They didn't throw away treasures. One didn't leave a door open for misunderstanding.

For lunch I prepared a cheese sandwich on wheat bread but left off the lettuce and condiments I usually added. I poured myself a glass of red wine, breaking a long stretch of not drinking before evening. I settled before the television to see what the midday news had to offer. I quickly became witness to ongoing riots in several cities, out-of-control disease, haranguing politicians and activists. Local shootings, robberies, and traffic crashes were covered, eventually giving way to long-winded description of the weather and tedious enthusiasm for professional sports. There'd eventually be a feel-good finisher about rooftop gardens, pandas, heroic acts etc., but by then I wasn't watching. I was gazing over the darkened screen, deciding whether to have another glass of wine, gradually giving in.

Glass replenished, I allowed myself to drift in the recliner. Somewhere in memory, in hermetically sealed containers stacked at the rearmost wall of my mind, I imagined the timeless positive moments in my life–the people, places, and things that at specific moments achieved balance with the toxic effluvia of human existence. My exposure to art, the sense of something higher that would dictate my tastes in films, music, and literature. Running through the crisp autumn air with my cross-country teammates, knowing the distinctness of a season now blurred, like the others, by climate debasement. The mastery of debate, of logic and correct language, its value in book discussions and bull sessions later. A number of outdoor concerts escorting young women in dresses, plays and restaurant dinners with other women, the occasional intimacy. A vision of the future, from rocket models in childhood to apparent opportunity out of college, before the full force of evil was known.

I suddenly realized that my eyes were closed, my head inclined forward toward my chest. A slight stiffness in my body confirmed that I'd napped. This won't do, I thought, there's that therapy session. I forced myself forward and up, looked dazedly about. There was just about time to get ready for work, be there in time for the session. On my desk was a list of topics for discussion with Rinai. I'd left space between the topics to add specific questions in discreet phraseology, but there wasn't time for that now. Taking pen in hand, I simply added question marks behind each topic heading, making it an open-ended inquiry to which Rinai could ramble in response. I could then cut in at will on points that interested me.

Arriving at the Center, I breezed straight along to the small conference room I'd reserved for our meeting. It was more formal than usual for such a session but I wanted to ensure Rinai took it seriously. I felt confident despite a lingering grogginess. On opening the door to the room, however, I found not only Rinai and Megan seated at the conference table, but Dr. Gruner and Midori in straight-back chairs along one wall. Observers, I realized, reason unknown.

"Proceed," the director smiled, Midori looking uncomfortable.

I settled in next to Megan, Rinai across the table from us. My plan for the questions seemed faulty now, though the original might have been worse, put me on the spot. But I shouldn't yield control to Rinai. I needed to spread the attention and accountability around. I huddled for a moment with Megan, speaking *sotto voce*.

"These are the general points we want to cover today. Ask her a general question on each one–'Tell us about,' etc., etc. I'll cut in when there's a detail I want. At the end say something encouraging to her."

"Okay."

I assumed the posture of a seasoned senior professional, though I had no idea if this would work. Megan was scanning the rough outline I'd handed her.

"Rinai," she began, "can you tell us how you were introduced to the Kakili cult? Was it through your father or other adults? Or did you go to the ceremonies and all on your own?"

Rinai gave me a glance, momentarily surprised by Megan being the questioner.

"I had many fathers," she said, "and many mothers, though I knew which bore me. I went to no ceremonies. The power, Kakili, was simply known, part of life."

"This power, the Kakili, how did it begin? And when, more or less? Do you believe that it's immortal?"

"We only know it is to be feared. It is the greatest power. It shares its power if we fear it. We express our fear through sacrifice."

"How do you get the specific abilities you want, and are you limited in how you can use them?"

"The powers wanted are defined in our prayers, the prayers of sacrifice, said in our language. Kakili has no limits. Power he lends goes on until he withdraws it."

"Tell us about Tapunui, where he came from, how you control him."

"I do not control him. He is a servant of Kakili, summoned by Sven."

"But he *killed* Sven!" I interjected. "Either him or you!"

Rinai eyed me stonily.

"No," she said.

"Go on," I said to Megan. "Next question."

"Are you under orders or duress of any kind from the headman of your tribe, Zel the priest-doctor, or the authorities of the autonomous zone?"

"No," Rinai replied.

"All right," I said to Megan. "I'll take over." She slid me the ersatz outline.

"Rinai," I said, "we need to know more about your sacrifices. You said they were to express your fear to the Kakili, that he lent you some of his power in return. But what is your purpose in obtaining this power? What plan do you have? And what is the ultimate goal of the Kakili?"

"We do not presume to know the Kakili's final plan for things. We only seek, at least *I* only seek, to serve him. What others plan by falsely seeking the power I do not know."

"But someone was using the power in Scania and killed people with it. Who could it be if not you? Sven would not use it to destroy *himself*. Someone wanted to gain from it and so killed with it. Who if not you?"

Rinai glanced toward the observers, her lips parted, hesitated a moment before speaking.

"The witch Tuva. She brought us together to please the Kakili, then used the power she gained to summon Tapunui. He was to destroy us so Tuva could steal the genes of our child for her own monstrous race, unborn babirusas awaiting her shock to life. She would guide them to look human, to believe in her supremacy, to serve her. It would please the Kakili, she thought, his own thirst for mayhem, but I discovered her plan because I know evil, I saw the babirusas. I made my own sacrifices and Tapunui became confused, then out of control."

"What about Frans?"

"He was simply a tool, one to support her as she studied the dark practices of many lands, disguised as innocent collecting."

"The later victims, Rinai, the one on the airplane and the ones around here. Tapunui was not present. Were those deaths your own doing?"

She was silent, glancing again toward Dr. Gruner and Midori.

"You can be truthful," I said. "This is a therapy session. Nothing said here can be used by police or courts."

"On the airplane I felt in danger, someone or something pursuing me. I sacrificed with herbs for protection but the Kakili struck the man sitting behind me, an innocent. The response of evil to supplication is often careless, misdirected. In the motel I only wanted the man restrained, but his life was taken. When I sacrificed in my room, desperate for company in the new place, another Tapunui was brought outside my window. He saw the guard and her gun, the fire of her cigarette, threw his much greater fire at her. With Amelia I did no sacrificing, I was upset and a little angry. I *was* then the Tapunui, unable to stop my actions as I forced her to the false suicide."

She looked down, perhaps with some sense of shame. We observed her in silence. I considered discussing Vic, decided it wasn't germane here. Her use of teleportation could be probed separately.

"Thank you for being open with us, Rinai. You'd probably like to rest now. Megan, will you please walk back with her?" Then, again *sotto voce*: "Lock her in."

They left. We waited as their footsteps receded. Dr. Gruner leaned forward in his chair.

"Well," he said, "I don't know about therapeutic value, but it was interesting. Definitely interesting."

"She got to vent anyway," Midori commented. "Some value there, it seems."

"Yes, of course. And in doing so she validated our having her here, the extremity of her case. To be able to help her would be unparalleled achievement. Question is, are we up to it?"

"We can deal with it as scientists and social therapists. But there are aspects maybe outside our purview. Teleporting?"

"Oh, it's in the ballpark theoretically. But of course, we're not quite that much into theory here."

"There's a unique consideration," I spoke up. "The abilities she's talking about would have evolved over many millennia, since long before scientific thought. The belief in hidden, all-powerful forces, reinforced among members of an isolated, primitive society, never challenged by critical thinking, might have instilled not only indelible fear but unshakeable confidence in the power of a hidden entity. The sacrifices to control its anger could in time have been seen to elicit benefits, first things they already had–good crops, successful hunting–but later things they desired–move large objects, destroy enemies. The collective will of all in the tribe, fueled by fear of Kakili but confidence in his power, would generate a psychic energy causing the evolution of abilities such as Rinai's."

Dr. Gruner blankly stared at me, Midori slightly smiling.

"So," the director said, "we are dealing then not with extreme dysfunction, but with extremely *efficient* functioning."

"Yes and no," I replied. "Extremely efficient in the ancient context in which it formed, but totally out of place and maladjusted in the modern world."

"The Department of Defense might not agree. I suspect they'd find plenty of use for her."

"But they don't have her," Midori pointed out. "We do. And she's a foreign national."

"Yes, that's true."

"Actually," I resumed, "the opportunity for us couldn't be better. We can work to normalize Rinai within society and the world, educating her about potential dangers with her abilities. Then we assist her in turning them toward positive, productive goals. An extreme dysfunction thus becomes a valuable resource for good purposes."

Gruner waited to see if I was finished.

"I like it," he said.

"Seems like you've nailed it," Midori added.

❦

As the evening passed and the night matron came on, the Center grew quiet and I was drawn to reflection. Rinai had presented herself as less culpable than we'd thought, near-blameless among forces that were not of her choosing. Yet, according to Zel, she'd been among the most active in her community, a clan that had sought empowerment from a known horror, the Kakili. He, more likely *it*, was apparently some other-dimensional and evil collective consciousness derived from the ancient "old ones," huge and terrible first inhabitants of the earth, now sealed beneath Antarctica. But why had Rinai's forebears, in response to their fears, chosen evil itself as their protection rather than a beneficent god, or a duality of good and evil? It implied a predisposition toward the less-than-human, the bestial, as if their evolutionary ancestor had been something distinct from most people's, perhaps the ancient babirusa. The alienation of Rinai and her clan, its disregard for other societies and their values, would then be far too deeply imbued to soon be changed.

There was a DNA test, I recalled, that I'd asked Midori to do on Rinai. She'd done it simultaneous with snake-boy's, hadn't quite finished, had found an anomaly in his but not in hers. Could the samples have been switched? But then, maybe it didn't matter. Over millions of years' evolution, the genetic configuration of Rinai's ancestors was no doubt altered by external factors. The babirusa marker had most likely atrophied.

I was getting carried away, I decided. I got up to stroll through the Center before finishing for the night.

Walking the halls, I noticed a couple of computer monitors left on, an eating disorder client sneaking food, a guard slumped over in the chapel. I turned off the monitors, pretended to not see the eater, checked to ensure the guard was sleeping, not dead. I was coming to enjoy these hours, the quiet, the leaving by midnight to return to Midori. I stopped in my walk by a window at the back, viewed our substantial grounds, the stark trees and ubiquitous snow. Winter was still with us, the March lion having just arrived. Continuing on, I passed Amelia's room, the black ribbon placed on the door by Helen, a reminder of my supposed disastrous negligence.

The next room was Rinai's, door of course closed at this time, perhaps locked. I stood by it imagining her inside, all that she'd said in the therapy session, the long road she'd taken to this place, this night. I became aware of a draft around my ankles, cool and then increasingly cold, striving to match the frigidity outdoors. I was perplexed. My complacent sense of peace and well-being had suddenly dissipated.

I tried the door. Locked.

Get help, I thought. Perhaps the guards.

I glanced up and down the hall. One guard in the chapel, asleep, Cpl. Colyer and another up front, far away and around turns. The others, who could say?

This couldn't wait.

I had a master key myself, took it from my pocket, opened the door and entered. It was dark and frostily cold inside, a smell like snow and something else. Smoke. I groped for a light switch and found it, illuminated the room. There was some disorder, things strewn around, but what garnered my full attention was a large, roughly bordered hole in the wall where the room's window should have been, non-opening since this had been a detention facility. I advanced to the hole and saw broken and melted glass, twisted pieces of frame, chunks of brick and mortar. The notorious blast of fire had once again been wielded, this time to effect escape. What had she teleported here? A lightning bolt? A jet engine thrust? Some military weapon? I could only guess since she had the entire world to choose from, and the universe beyond.

X.

I naturally called Dr. Gruner at his home, the first time I had done so. We agreed to delay involving the police since, anyway, they usually required a 24-hour absence before taking a missing person report. Of course, there was also serious property damage and Rinai had confessed a murder to us, but we could pay for repairs without an insurance claim and the confession was privileged information. There were other considerations, such as her immigration status and the remote possibility she'd been kidnapped, but we didn't find these pressing. Our overwhelming concern was the jeopardy into which the Center had been placed, a danger brought about by extreme dysfunction.

I called Midori and briefly explained why I'd be late, then talked with Cpl. Colyer and by phone with Sgt. Hendon, bringing them into our plan for discretion. They were agreeable, not wishing reassignment to more hazardous posts. We moved furniture against the hole in Rinai's room, reduced the heat to minimum, plugged the draft around the door with plastic trash bags. I left a phone message for our maintenance contractor, giving them first shot at the repair job. I departed about two hours later than usual.

I entered the apartment and the bedroom quietly, Midori appearing to be asleep. She wasn't, however.

"So what will happen now?" she asked in the dark.

"I guess we'll wait and see. I'll come in earlier tomorrow. Maybe you can let them know."

"Operations to be normal?"

"We're going to try for it. Of course, a lot is up in the air just now."

"Maybe she'll come back."

"That'd be great. Wish I could believe it."

"You don't think so?"

"Not going by the hole she left. Wait till you see it."

"Hm. Fear. A powerful reaction to it. Yet why should she be that afraid? You let her off

easy in the session."

"Not compared to the folks in Scania. They coddled her like a princess, until they had the chance to dump her."

"You don't regret taking her, though. Right?"

"Yeah, she was a big hope for the Center. We shouldn't have let so much hinge on her, though. She was always a gamble, a speculation. Then too, I had my own agenda, right alongside the Center's. Bart will no doubt blame me if this ruins us. Maybe he'll be right."

"No, don't say that now. Your agenda was a good one. Vital, important to all of us. And it still is."

"Thank you."

"With Bart, just remind him it was John brought the case in, not you."

❦❦❦

I returned to the Center immediately after lunch, my apprehension growing. Sgt. Hendon greeted me cordially, apparently well in control of things. As I proceeded through the building, however, I sensed a malaise settling over its occupants. An out-patient addiction group, Bart's responsibility, was sitting around his and Helen's office watching a sports talk show on TV. I saw other clients wandering about, then the reincarnated Egyptian princess chattering at Rachel, who listened distractedly and gave me a half-hearted wave. I felt a flicker of regret towards her. My mood changed as a bustling figure entered my field of vision. Rudy. I slowed and awaited his habitual enthusiasm, not unwelcome now.

"She hasn't come back," he bluntly informed me.

"Rinai?"

"Yeah."

"Well, we'll hope for the best."

"Do you think she's dead?"

"That certainly wouldn't be for the best."

"Yeah."

"By the way, I noticed an unsupervised addiction group in Bart's office, watching some junk TV."

"Right. He tells me to watch them while he he goes off to rap with Gruner. Like I'm his coolie or something."

"Bart did that?"

"Yeah. He's getting to be a real–but listen, where do you stand?"

"Stand? On what?"

"Bart's thing about closing if your client doesn't come back. That's what he's pushing Gruner on."

"Close the Center? Seems rather hasty. Very rash, in fact."

"So you're against it?"

"Of course!"

"Me, too. I'm just turning the corner with Luke, might be a full cure. Well, I'll go check on Bart's addicts."

He gave me a collegial pat on the arm and hastened off down the hall. It occurred to me that his Luke, alias snake-boy, might inherit Rinai's mantle of "signature client," since

Amelia too was out of the picture. It was hard to imagine Dr. Gruner and Rudy presenting him to the public, insisting they had instilled human nature in a beast, but who could say? I resolved to remain no part of it.

I continued down the hallway to Rinai's damaged room. Arriving there, I found a contractor and two assistants at work on the hole, and Midori inspecting a pile of swept-up rubble. She was using a magnifying glass and seemed fascinated by what she saw.

"Look at this," she said, and handed me a misshapen gray stone.

"What about it?"

"It's igneous rock, recent in origin."

"Igneous, so–volcanic?"

"You got it," she smiled. "There's a bunch of them."

I was silent and no doubt looked amazed as I tried to envision Rinai blasting her way through the wall.

"Seems there's no limit," Midori observed, "when our girl gets to teleporting."

<hr />

Over 24 hours had passed and Rinai had not returned. She hadn't made contact and there was no word about her, so Dr. Gruner made a missing person report to the police. He gave only the most basic facts, her identifying information and the time and place of her disappearance. He said nothing about the reasons for her treatment, her admitted past actions, or the hole in the wall. It was understood that an effective search might involve a public announcement, photos on television and such. Dr. Gruner asked that they delay that part, suggesting it might alarm the client if she saw it, induce panic.

"Well, that's done," he said as he hung up the phone. "I

suppose we'll have to show them the wall eventually. How are the repairs coming?"

"The brickwork was kind of tricky," I replied, "but it's setting now. They say the window work will go fast. Then there's the plastering and paint."

"Such destruction. Was she sending us a message, do you think?"

"Could be. But, judging from her own words and from what I've seen, I think it's more likely a force out of control. The indiscriminate nature of evil, or of power derived from it."

Dr. Gruner shook his head.

"Whatever made us think we could work with her?"

We were both silent a moment.

"It must be stopped," the director stated.

"It will be," I said. "It has to be."

⊜⊷⦕⧢⊶⦖⧢⊶⧢⊷⦕⊷⧢

Despite Dr. Gruner's request, the public was quickly made aware of Rinai's flight, then of the hole blasted in the wall, courtesy of someone's "smart phone" photo. Several clients with lesser disorders immediately withdrew and a couple of support staff quit. Dr. Gruner was kept busy reassuring contributors and dispelling rumors with the media, including one about terrorist infiltration. There was tacit agreement that I should lie low, having been both Rinai's worker and the person in charge at the time of her breakout. I therefore kept to myself around the Center, limiting my work to the search for Rinai and my hope for expungement of the evil she represented. I had the passwords for her credit card account, which was billed to the Center, and accessed it on the Internet trying to determine her flight path. She'd

166

completed only one transaction since her escape, however, obtaining her maximum cash advance from a local ATM.

I talked with Rachel, her former worker, about places Rinai might have gone. Rachel could only name the shops and cheap restaurants they had visited on their outings. I did the tour of these places, showing Rinai's photo, but only one or two people had recollections of her, and those vague and not recent. I stayed in contact with the police, but they too came up with nothing. People at the Center were moving on to other concerns, chief among them their own financial futures. They were becoming resigned to the loss of Rinai as a client, envisioning its effects on the Center and their own employment.

"He's set a meeting for this afternoon," Midori informed me, referring to Dr. Gruner. "Charter members and observers, you included."

"Who are the others?"

"The aides and Lucia."

"The psychiatric nurse?"

"Seems he wants all the professionals."

"Sounds like a personnel issue."

"Hope not."

I duly attended the meeting, sitting with the other observers in straight-backed chairs against the wall, the members reclining at the conference table. There was a nervous silence until everyone was seated, Dr. Gruner and Bart shuffling notes, others doodling. An officious clearing of throat finally broke the silence.

"The purpose of this meeting," our director intoned, "is as follows: It has been moved and seconded among the charter members that the Center for Integrative Treatment of Extreme Dysfunction be closed. All financial outlay beyond payment of existing obligations would cease immediately. Current resident clients would be transferred back to their referring entities or to alternative resources, public or charitable."

Dr. Gruner hesitated, looked up from the sheet he'd been reading from, scanned the faces in the room.

"Do you care to elaborate, Bart? Or shall we proceed to questions and the vote?"

"I'll elaborate, of course."

Our colleague then launched into an attack on the organization and management of the Center, including the absences of Dr. Gruner and myself, and the selection of cases for acceptance, leading to our lack of success in treatment, culminating in disaster. He continued with a claim of financial chaos, uncontrolled spending and mounting debts, citing the example of Rinai's ATM withdrawal. Financial support would collapse due to bad publicity, leaving the Center's viability in tatters, along with the reputations of its professionals.

"It's time to close up shop," Bart insisted, "minimize the damage."

There was an interval of silence when he finished, Helen looking triumphant, Rudy shifting about but slow to form a rebuttal. The observers weren't supposed to speak, but I heard Lucia muttering.

"What about those of us with children?" she called out. "We can't just be out on the street!"

It suddenly occurred to me that none of us, except Lucia apparently, had children in our homes. Ours was a rarefied world, emotionally and spiritually distant to allow clinical dissection of abnormalities among the herd.

"Severance packages will be processed," Bart replied crisply, "with what capital can be salvaged."

"What about those clients? You can't just dump them!"

Bart deferred to Dr. Gruner.

"Lucia, I'm sorry," the director said, "but discussion must be limited to charter members only. We can talk privately later if you like."

The nurse retreated unhappily. Rudy cleared his throat and leaned into the table across from Bart.

"It seems to me all we've heard are negatives about our situation. Actually, we've had some successes. *I've* seen some anyway. And we've really got a lot going for us. We've got a pool of talent that, if properly used–"

He was interrupted in mid-gesture by the door opening, one of the secretaries looking in and around the room, settling on Dr. Gruner.

"Excuse me. There's an emergency phone call for Mr. Padraig."

"Who?" asked the confused director.

The secretary read off a slip of paper in her hand: "P-A-D-R-A-I-G."

A buried memory suddenly surfaced in my mind.

"That's for me!" I blurted, my curiosity stirred. "I'll take it."

I left them all wondering as I rose and followed the secretary out the door. It felt good to escape the straight-backed chair and the tense meeting. We continued down the hall and into the clerical pool.

"Should I transfer it to your office?"

"No, I'll take it here." I didn't want to risk disconnection. "Hello, Mr. Patel?"

"Yes, Mr. Padraig. I am here. Also, I have Rinai."

"You *what*?"

"I have Rinai, the missing person of your acquaintance. And I have informed no one except you."

"How did you get involved in this?"

"We can discuss that later. Time is of the essence now. I'm not sure how long I can keep her."

"Keep her as long as you possibly can. Where are you?"

"I will tell you, Padraig, but for both our sakes you must tell no one else. And I need you to bring something to me."

"What is it?"

"A small object in your possession, or perhaps a colleague's. A certain fetish you carried off from Scania. A little horn."

"The ancient babirusa tusk?"

"That would be it, with a hole."

"All right. But why do you need it?"

"To resolve the problems with Rinai, and hopefully with the Kakili. We are on the same side, Padraig."

I hesitated, wondering if this were true.

"On the plane, Patel, you said to trust no one."

"I believe I said some others would say that. I myself would leave the door open for times when there is little choice. This is such a time and more, when an all-consuming evil threatens our world."

I recalled the death of John, the glare of Tapunui, the baby babirusas in jars, the hole from volcanic blast.

"Okay," I said. "Give me the address."

※⸙≫⸙※

Since I'd left the ancient tusk with Midori, I needed to extract her from the meeting to obtain it. Returning to the conference room, I edged up to her chair as softly as possible while Bart and Rudy argued about cross-species transference, Rudy's specialty which Bart now called "California quackery." Gaining Midori's attention with a shoulder touch, I leaned in to whisper over the bickering.

"I have a chance to pick up Rinai, but I need that old babirusa tusk. I need you to get it right now and not tell anyone."

She slipped out of her chair and we exited the room, Rudy distracting from our departure with claims of success working with snake-boy. Midori stepped briskly down the hallway to the lab, I keeping pace, thankful she didn't delay with conversation. It seemed I felt closest to her under pressure. She was soon unlocking the metal specimen cabinet, poking among the contents, withdrawing a plastic vial containing the tusk. She handed it to me as if it were gold, though its value we knew was much greater.

"I'm going with you," she said.

"I don't know if that's–"

"I'm not letting you out of my sight."

Her eyes were intense, all casualness gone.

"They'll want you in the meeting, for the vote."

"I'll send in an absentee ballot. Hold on."

She turned to a counter and grabbed a pen and notepad, wrote "I vote NO" with her signature and the date.

"All right, let's get our coats."

She gave the note to the secretary who'd summoned me from the meeting, told her to take it directly to Dr. Gruner. Outside, we took my car and headed west across the far northern fringe of suburbs, the address being in a nearly rural area of large properties with stately homes. After a time there few stop lights and higher speed limits, a general lack of commerce. It would be unlit for driving at night.

"Thought it'd be in the city," Midori commented.

"Yeah, she must be in somebody's house."

"Or else a farm."

"Possible. Though I can't picture that for the contact."

"Who was–?"

"A man I met on the plane. Gave the name Patel, no doubt a pseudo, as mine was supposed to be."

"The one called out at the meeting? Padraig, was it?"

"Right. Gaelic translation."

"Okay. Still, he was able to find you, know your link to Rinai. But I guess she might've clued him in."

"Actually, he'd seen me with her before. On the earlier flight, when I first brought her over."

"Oh? Wow, that's interesting."

"How, especially?"

"Well, it's quite a coincidence he was on both flights with you. Mathematically remote. He was either after her himself or protecting her. And there's no reason to guess the latter since she wasn't with you on the second flight."

"Hm. Come to think of it, Rinai said she used the Kakili's power on the plane because she felt she was being pursued. Of course, then it misfired and killed the man behind her."

"So this Patel was lucky."

"So it would seem."

"And now today he turns the tables."

I soon turned off the fast road onto an unlined, little traveled one. It was flanked by huge lawns or pastures with widely spaced mansions set well back in them. The occasional horse stared at us from behind white-painted enclosure. A few minutes more brought us to an even smaller road, little more than a driveway, branching off to the right. A tiny street sign indicated that it led to our destination. I turned in and drove very slowly along the winding, hilly, heavily forested little road. There were attractive houses visible through the growth, still spaced widely but not on a plane with the mansions we'd seen. There were mailboxes by the road with address numbers, but many were difficult to read in the failing light or else missing digits. The road petered out into a gravel turnaround where we sat with the engine idling, the sky a darkening gray, the air gaining chill toward freezing.

"We must have missed it," I stated flatly.

"Nothing to do but have another go," Midori added.

"Yeah, we'll see the other sides of the boxes better."

I put the car in gear and we started back. We hadn't gone far, however, before we noticed a mailbox with numbers attached vertically on its post. They matched our sought-after address. I pulled into the crescent-shaped driveway and parked behind a black van that was sitting well short of the house entrance. Occupants of my car would not be visible from a window.

"I think you should stay here," I told Midori. "If you don't hear from me in thirty minutes, call the police and tell them Rinai is here and someone is in danger."

"Okay, sure. Good luck."

It fleetingly seemed we should kiss, but I was already exiting the car and my focus was on the house. I saw one sprawling level, windows all with closed curtains, old-fashioned weather vane on the roof. I advanced to the stoop, pressed the doorbell, heard no ring inside. I tried it once more, then rapped with vigor on the glass storm door. I heard noises of approach, some pulling on the door, and there was Patel, looking much as he had on our flights together. He wasn't smiling, but we shook hands and he drew me in, albeit with a hint of anxiety.

"I have her downstairs," he said.

"What, there's a basement?"

"No. Here, I'll show you."

Entering the house, I saw a full dining room to the left of the vestibule, a kitchen no doubt beyond. To my right was a large living room, conventionally furnished, a hallway leading further to the right. On the near side of the living room was a carpeted descending staircase. Patel led me to it and down to a lower level, where we entered another sizable living room. This one had a fireplace with a gas-fed fire on low, trendy furniture, and a billiard table in front of a picture window with its view of twilight enfolding a bare-limbed forest.

"The house is built into a hillside," Patel explained. "Where you entered is actually the second floor."

"This is your home base?"

"No, it belongs to the consortium."

"Your employer?"

"So to speak. Contractual work on behalf of a member. She did much damage before you or your friends knew her."

"I had no idea."

"Of course. How could you? She is an avatar, naturally pleasing in form and manner for purposes of deception."

"But she was born, had a mother and father, I think."

"How can you know? Coming from the place she does, countless generations of worshipers of evil. Millennia of collective will against the laws of matter."

"Are there others like her?"

"Not on her level. Without her, the one she calls Kakili will shrink back into his cocoon. If we let her escape, earth's misery increases tenfold."

"How are you able to keep her here?"

"I made promises, brought her here by the fire, used a variety of hypnosis. One who depends on evil for power is essentially ignorant, therefore vulnerable to other suggestions. But my control of her is limited, so we must act. Have you brought the fetish?"

I reached into my coat and brought out the vial containing the well-traveled little tusk.

"I don't see how this will be fatal to her," I said as I gave it to him.

"Oh, we do not want to kill her. To martyr someone is to disperse their power to others, perhaps greatly expanded."

"Well, what then?"

"You will see. Wait here while I bring her. She is in one of the guest rooms. They are windowless since the rear of this floor is enclosed by earth."

He disappeared into a dim passage. I took the opportunity to phone Midori out in the car.

"Better make that sixty minutes on the police call. I don't know how long this will take."

"Sure. But are you okay? Give me a hint if you're not."

"No problem. If you get cold, there are blankets in the trunk. Try not to run the motor."

"Okay, fine."

"I have to click off."

Patel came back leading Rinai by one arm. She paid me no attention as he led her to the middle of a couch facing the fire. He had her sit. She was wearing an oversized turquoise robe, probably left by a previous guest, and her long hair was untied. She was, at that moment, quite innocent to my eyes, entirely undeserving of whatever was to happen to her. But I was reduced now to an observer's role, and what I saw was the culmination of my own quest, my goal since the death of John. Not revenge, nor an isolated application of justice, but the defeat of a widespread evil at the root of so much human suffering.

Patel knelt before her, light from the fire flickering behind him, and spoke in the dialect I'd heard in Rinai's village. He then produced the ancient babirusa tusk, taking it from the plastic vial and holding it before her. He spoke to her further, greater earnestness in his tone. He placed the fetish in Rinai's cupped hands and slowly withdrew to one side, the firelight now falling full upon her. He made two or three more short statements, very firm, as he drew away, finally taking my own arm and leading me away from the scene.

We were in a utility and storage room that I judged to be under the dining room upstairs. There was a personal computer and writing desk in one corner, an abstract art print hung on the wall above them. Patel remained focused on the room we'd just left, calm but alert as we watched the passageway.

"We will be safe here from repercussions," he said. "She is presently accessing the power of the Kakili to transport herself and the fetish to Inner Earth. Those were my orders to her, though results and side effects can be unpredictable."

"How long will she remain down in the earth?"

"Until after the next Ice Age, unless she gets lucky and is reached by a volcanic seam, which then will spew her essence over the surface."

"And the Kakili?"

"He will be cowering down there with her, his power severely reduced since turned against itself in the teleportation. The added power instilled in the fetish will be unexpected and disastrous on his end."

"What about his followers still up here? Their abilities derived from fervent belief in evil?"

"They will find their abilities much diminished since the agent for them is removed. Their loyalty to him will flag, their sacrifices grow less fervent, their belief weaken."

"And the Kakili's own power derives from their belief."

"Belief that is fear."

"Although fear could grow again, could it not, among the ignorant? Enough perhaps to resurrect the Kakili? Or engender a new one?"

"Fear is inherent, Padraig, in the human condition. And ignorance is indeed encroaching on the civilized world. But at least it can be controlled through conventional means, as long as there is the will. There needn't be adventures like ours tonight."

"Speaking of which, when do we check on her?"

"We will do so now."

Patel and I moved through the passageway and back into the flicker of firelight. Rinai's form was not visible above the back of the couch. We continued ahead and towards the fire, saw that the couch was not empty. The robe she'd been wearing lay in folds as if collapsed from a disappearing body. Atop the robe was the ancient tusk, appearing slightly shrunken and a shade darker in color, the appearance of having been cooked. Patel endeavored to pick it up for inspection, but it broke into fragments between his fingers. I knelt down to gather some of the fragments, but they crumbled into dust as I handled them.

"There was conflict," Patel said, "resistance by the power in the fetish to being teleported by a later, derivative power. The old ones will not be usurped, even by their horrific posterity. The latter's offense must result in ruin for them, or at least great loss, and thus a reprieve for their potential victims."

"And Rinai?"

"She is gone as I described to you."

He again took my arm and led me to the stairway. We ascended to the vestibule where I'd entered.

"I must now attend to clean-up," he said, "and communicate with the consortium. I trust you will keep the particulars of this episode in confidence. It is to both of our advantages."

We shook hands and he opened the door for me.

"Just one question," I said.

"Yes?"

"Why did you play chess so poorly on the plane?"

He shrugged.

"It was good for getting to know you."

❧❦❧

I found Midori wrapped in a couple of blankets, phone in hand.

"Good we had those," I said. "Sorry it took so long."

"Where's Rinai?"

"I'll talk as I drive."

I felt as if I were describing a dream as I gave my account of what had happened in the house. Driving past the upscale properties, then on the fast road, I was unloading what had to seem an unreality, yet receiving vindication from my professional and personal partner. Still wrapped in the blankets, she asked few questions, processing the facts along with myself. As we approached a pub I'd noticed on the way

177

out, its attractive yellow sign with Gothic lettering, I suggested we stop for a drink. Midori readily agreed.

Seated inside at a heavy oaken table, my companion checking her phone messages, I reflected that John would have liked this place, enjoyed discussing the case. Things had changed so unpredictably, yet that must be expected when one involves himself in extremes of experience. He gives up the safety of routines, the laws, the warnings of civilized society.

"I got a text from Megan," Midori said. "The Center survived, four votes to two. Bart and Helen resigned after the meeting."

"So snake-boy still has a home. Great. Good to hear."

"Yes, it is." A hesitation, then: "What if the police showed up *now*? Back there, back at the house?"

"They'd find no trace of anything. An employee of the owners if he hasn't already left. A turquoise robe hung in a bedroom, some powdered babirusa bone committed to the winds or flushed down a toilet."

"An ignominious end."

"Well deserved, as it is by all purveyors of evil."

"Agreed once again." And, with a smile: "But what about us? Think we came out ahead after everything?"

I gave her a searching look, saw her clearly apart from all clutter.

"I've been meaning to tell you something, Dr. Tateyama: I find you beautiful."

I raised my stein of dark beer, and she hers, the glass making cautious contact in the pub's gentle firelight.

EPILOGUE

Dear Assistant Director:
There have been recent events here which may be of interest to you, involving as they do parties with whom it seems you are familiar.

A deportee we recently received, one Tapunui, has disappeared despite our scrupulous attention to him. (You are listed as a witness in his prosecution.) A vigorous and continuing search (including within the autonomous zone) has not produced him. All points of departure from the island have been blocked to him since his arrival.

At the same time as this disappearance, a young woman who had emigrated was found wandering through her former village in the autonomous zone. She was uncommunicative, possibly amnesiac, but was recognized by some of the villagers as one Rinai. She was left in the care of her purported mother and one Zel, the village medical practitioner, who claimed to have professional ties to you.

I believe these matters will soon be laid to rest. If inquiries arise from other sources, however, I trust we will be mutually supportive in our responses.

Respectfully,
Capt. Ravi Edward
Royal National Police Force